Loving Jake

by

Lisa Lanay

Loving Jake © 2019 Lisa Lanay

Published by Lisa Lanay
www.lisalanay.com
Instagram @lisalanayauthor
FB @lisalanayauthor

Book cover by Eva Talia Designs
(http://evataliadesigns.com)

To the friends who have encouraged me to pursue my passion throughout the years.
I appreciate your endless support, manuscript reading, and feedback:
Jim Cozzi, Mary Beth Baskin, Gail Olson, Karen Gleason, Maria Urbinati, Cindy Wohlberg, Kathy O'Brien, Kathy Tudisco, Kim McCarthy, Shannon Riley, Ruth Waters,
& with love to my son Joey who assisted in making the dream come alive for me.

Thank you.

Hugs and kisses to each of you, always.

Chapter 1

Jake drove past the large Tudor home before parking next to the curb and shutting off the car's engine. Had it really been four years since he had attended one of George Urbane's infamous Fourth of July parties? Four years since he had last seen friends whom he once considered his closest in the world? He didn't question why he had lost contact with the people he had considered family because he knew the answer. He knew all too well why he had had to leave, had to escape.

A familiar churning deep in his gut threatened to surface as he stared out the car's side window, lost in a past better off forgotten. The day four years ago had been warm and pleasant, as was typical for Northern California in July. Over a hundred people had gathered for the annual celebration where the hors d'oeuvres were plentiful and the alcohol flowed freely, probably too freely, as several of the guys had ended up in the swimming pool by mid-afternoon wearing grass skirts with nothing underneath them. Some things you can never un-see, he acknowledged with a grin teasing the corner of his lips.

His thoughts sobered; it had also been one of those rare occasions that he and Brenda had not argued for most of the afternoon, at least not until George and Linda had made their announcement. They were expecting their second child. The second in two years.

The last he had heard from a source he couldn't recall, his ex and her husband had two children and had moved to Arizona. She had found someone to provide her with what he could never give her, could give no woman. "I hope you're happy, Brenda," he whispered.

Shocked to realize he held the steering wheel in a death grip, he released his hands, mentally shaking from his mind the disturbing images of the past. Although his heart beat faster than normal, he was ready to go to the party and reunite with his friends. He was determined to leave the past where it belonged, in the past, and enjoy himself this afternoon. He retrieved a bottle of Cabernet from the trunk with a brief glance at the label. The name of a French winery was prominently embossed at the top. A grin curled the corner of his lips. George and Linda, like many of his friends, liked to boast that California wines were equal to French ones, and Jake liked to provoke them whenever he had the chance.

He brushed a wayward strand of hair from his forehead and placed his sunglasses on top of his head. His eyes flickered over the many cars lining the street. He recognized none of them. The flashy sports cars, that were once he and his friends' sole preference for transportation, were gone. Range Rovers and Mercedes Crossovers stood in their place. Laughter bubbled inside of him. "Family vehicles." He chuckled with a glance over his shoulder at the Ferrari, gazing fondly upon the expensive sports car, and was grateful it had only two doors and would never be considered a cross between a station wagon and anything else.

He strode down the sidewalk, his long legs revealed in a pair of chino shorts. The normal cowboy swagger that women watched longingly as he reported from around the globe was less obvious in a pair of shorts and leather sandals than when he wore his usual worn jeans and snakeskin boots.

Jake drew in a long breath of air before ringing the doorbell of the familiar two-story home.

***

"My biological clock is not ticking! I'm only thirty-one years old; I have plenty of time to have kids," Kimberly exclaimed in exasperation. She looked at her sister and then over to Catherine, the wife of one of their brother's best friends, who only shrugged in response, and then back at her sister. Why couldn't Carly understand that not everyone needed to get married and have children before they were thirty as she had done. Her sister had chastised her the previous evening for not planning to bring a date to their brother's annual Fourth of July party, and even though Kimberly had enthusiastically explained that she did not need male companionship to enjoy a party, Carly wasn't convinced. As far as Carly was concerned, her older sister couldn't possibly be happy without any prospects for walking down the aisle in her near future.

It wasn't as if she didn't date, Kimberly mentally defended herself, a deep scowl crinkling her forehead, but then, she forced herself to admit, she really didn't. It's just that she preferred to think of it as more of an extended, self-imposed, sexual dry spell, rather than her inability to meet a guy she was even remotely interested in. A cold shiver slid over her skin as she recalled two of the men she had dated in the past five years, each for much longer than should be considered mentally sane. Besides, she rationalized, she didn't want to worry about entertaining someone when her family members did their best to take advantage of her photography skills, insisting she take plenty of photos during the party.

"Of course, I wouldn't turn down mind-blowing sex with—" she mumbled and then halted in mid-sentence because something had diverted her sister's attention elsewhere and Carly was no longer listening to her. "Carly, hello? Earth to Carly."

"Wow. Don't look now Kimberly, but I think the man to provide you with mind-blowing sex just walked in," Carly exclaimed excitedly.

Half afraid of what she would find, Kimberly twisted her head to look over her shoulder at what, or rather to whom, her sister referred. And as quickly as she had turned, she spun back around again. Only now her heart threatened to pound out of her chest, and her mouth gaped open, and, for the life of her, she couldn't seem to shut it.

Jake Taylor was here.
At her brother's house.
At his annual Fourth of July party.
After four years.
Here.
Jake Taylor.
Jake.
Here, and the one man who had the ability to stir the passion within her with something as simple as a smile or a glance from his warm hazel eyes. The one man she had loved for almost twenty years.

"What is going on? What's gotten into the two of you?" Catherine, the third in their trio, piped up.

"Jake Taylor just walked in. He's one of George's best friends, and he's also a friend of your husband's. He was out of the country last year and missed your wedding. Kimberly's been in love with him since the eighth grade." Carly moved to the edge of her seat, sat up straight, and peered over Catherine's shoulder at the party's newest arrival.

"I have not. How could you say such a thing?" Kimberly quickly sputtered, but not fast enough to prevent a heated blush from creeping up her neck and cheeks.

"Kimberly, give me and everyone else a break. You followed the guy around like a lovesick puppy as a kid. It wasn't much better when we got older, only then you hung on his every word as if it was gospel. Everyone knew how you felt about Jake."

"They did?" Kimberly searched her sister's face for signs of her earlier teasing and found none. "Even Jake?"

"Of course, he did. He would have had to have been blind not to." Carly waved her hand in a sweeping gesture.

She couldn't have been that obvious, could she? Oh, who was she kidding? she inwardly cringed. The smug expression on Carly's face confirmed it. Jake had known how she felt about him all this time, and it hadn't mattered because he had never been interested in her. She was George's little sister to him and nothing else. Always and forever the little sister. If Catherine hadn't grabbed Kimberly's arm, she would have made a run for it. And from Carly's knowing expression, she knew it too.

"Okay you two, what gives? You know I'm the new kid on the block and don't have a single ounce of dirt on anyone. So, spill it. I want details. Especially if you think this guy is a potential candidate to offer up mind-blowing sex. I will want details on that also, after the fact. Never hurts to learn a new thing or two," Catherine added pointedly, with a smirk in Kimberly's direction.

Kimberly blew away a long curl of hair that had fallen into her eyes with an air of defeat. Two of the most persistent people she knew stared back at her, and she didn't have a chance of avoiding the subject of Jake Taylor. She took a deep breath and decided, as Catherine eloquently put it, to spill it.

"Fine, you want details, here they are." Kimberly glared at her sister and her amused expression, before she turned her back on her to face Catherine.

8

"Jake lived down the street from us. He's George's age. I've sort of had a crush on him for a while." She avoided a glance at her sister because she was likely doing something as juvenile as rolling her eyes. "Anyway, I was, and always will be, George's little sister to him, four years his junior. Jake dated, married, and divorced, without a second glance in my direction. Period. End of story." Hearing herself say it out loud, she realized that she had held on to a bunch of foolish hopes and dreams all these years and it was time to let go of them.

"How can you say that?" Carly shrieked, her disbelief clear in her ear-piercing wail. "You never even let him know how you felt, at least not directly. The few times he tried to talk to you, you ran in the opposite direction as fast as you could."

Kimberly gripped the edge of the table and dug her fingernails into the soft wood. "What does it matter, anyway? You said yourself that he has always known how I felt about him. He wasn't interested in me then, and he won't be now."

Carly shook her head. "Wow, for a social influencer, with over twenty-thousand followers on Instagram, you sure are down on yourself."

Kimberly's eyes bulged wide. "I post photos of things I find interesting," she shot back in a whispered hiss. "That doesn't mean I have this unrealistic view of life. My life, specifically. I'm not going to humiliate myself by making a play for Jake, and you aren't going to try anything either. Promise me, Carly."

Carly's snort shot through Kimberly like a bunch of tiny pins sticking into her skin. "Kimberly, you were a teenager, and when you finally grew up and graduated college, he had already hooked up with his ex. That's changed now; you're all grown up, and he's available again. From the gossip I've gathered over the last couple of years, he's been wrapped up in his career, and according to *People* magazine last month, he's not in a serious relationship." Carly turned to Catherine and added, "He's an international correspondent, kind of like Anderson Cooper, only hipper, which is pretty amazing since Anderson Cooper is hip." She looked at her sister and placed her hand on her upper arm. "Kim, come on," Carly said encouragingly, "he's not involved with anyone. This could be your chance to—"

"Um, excuse me," interrupted Catherine with a nervous laugh. "But if the subject of our discussion is still the guy who is about six-foot-two, sun- bleached hair, and a body that could definitely offer mind-blowing sex, and a lot of it, then I'd say we have about two minutes before he's standing in front of us!"

Kimberly gasped. There was a flock of butterflies partying down in her stomach, and it felt as if a few of them may have made their way to her throat and were looking for an exit. A quick check over her sister's shoulder confirmed her worse fears. Jake was headed in a path that led him straight to them.

So much for escaping before he noticed our trio, she thought glumly. If she hadn't spent so much time trying to defend herself, she could be inside George's house right now, hiding in a bedroom closet, or better yet, making a beeline for the front door. She chewed nervously on her bottom lip. Had she remembered to put on make-up this morning? What about deodorant? Had she remembered to put on deodorant before darting off to run errands before the party? Yeah right, sure she did. She bent her head and discreetly sniffed each armpit. Why me? She groaned inwardly right before a voice from the past shot through her, sending every butterfly in her stomach into massive chaos.

"Hello, ladies."

"Jake!" Carly scrambled out of her chair and into his arms as fast as her very pregnant body allowed her. "I

10

didn't know you were coming! When did you arrive? Have you seen George yet?"

"Carly, you haven't changed at all, have you? Still shy as ever." Jake laughed in a deep, thick, sexy tone that replaced the earlier pin pricks with chills, skating along Kimberly's skin. "Except, maybe, for that little basketball you're now sporting."

"Due next month." Carly smiled proudly with a pat to her protruding stomach. "Jake," she continued, "I would like to introduce you to Catherine Sinclair, Rick's wife. They married last year."

"It's a pleasure to meet you Catherine."

Carly tilted her head toward her sister. "And, of course, you remember Kimberly?"

Kimberly watched the warmth of his smile spread across his lips, and she licked her own in response. He was more handsome than she remembered, his sun-bronzed skin smooth with only thin creases at the corner of his eyes when he smiled, his hair a shade lighter than brown, thick and pulled back from his face by a leather band at his nape. She looked into his eyes and found him staring at her, the honey-colored irises reflecting something close to amusement. Her eyes grew wide, and she quickly moved them to the region of his chest.

"Of course, I remember Kimberly." His playful grin, widened. "Just because you have dominated everyone's attention your entire life," he said to Carly, "doesn't mean I forgot you have a sister," he teased.

Kimberly glanced up at him again from her seat at the table, and still he stared at her. She swallowed, twice.

"It's nice to see you again, Kimberly."

"Um. Hi, Jake?" She twisted her hands together on her lap. "How are you?" she croaked in barely more than a whisper and then inwardly cringed. She tried to cool the blush that stained her neck and cheeks with several discreet waves of her hand, but she failed miserably. She glanced at her sister, and Carly's eyes glared back an unsubtle threat: make your move, sis, or I'll do the moving for you. Beneath the table, Kimberly wiped her damp palms on the front of her sundress and squeezed each of her trembling knees. All she wanted to do was dive under the table and pretend that she was invisible. Wholly crap, she inwardly moaned, if Jake really knew her feelings for him, how could she ever look him in the eye again? Especially when she wore the words *hopelessly in love with you* stamped on her forehead?

"Jake, please, have a seat. Have you eaten anything yet?" Carly shot a glaring look at Kimberly again and then diverted her attention back to Jake.

"Yes, I did. More that I should have." He patted the base of his abdomen, and his hands revealed a tight, flat stomach. "Five minutes after I walked in the door, Linda made sure I piled my plate high."

"That's Linda for you," Carly responded.

Kimberly pushed the pasta into a mound on her plate until a jolt of pain shot through the middle of her shin. "Ow," she muttered and rubbed her leg. Had her sister really just kicked her under the table with the tip of her Jimmy Choo platforms? She stole a glance at Carly, who responded with a meaningful glare.

"I'm glad you made it to the party. It has to be at least three years since we've seen you. The last I heard you were in Central America?" Carly prompted.

"South America, actually."

"It's been four years," Kimberly softly corrected, immediately causing the other three heads at the table to turn swiftly in her direction. "I, ah, went through some of George's Fourth of July photo albums not too long ago," she fumbled through the explanation despite the flush that crept up her neck and over her cheeks.

How Jake, and only Jake, had been able to capture her heart and then fluster her to the point of embarrassment because of it, had caused her more than one headache. She had met a lot of men in college, and later at various jobs, and never did any of them cause her heart to throb erratically the way Jake did. She would ask herself why, only to be reminded of the numerous times she had witnessed him going out of his way to be kind to someone, or how he always thought to bring flowers to her mother when invited to dinner, and she would know all too well the answer. He was probably more successful than most of his friends, yet he never bragged, and he always made everyone feel special, that whatever you did was of equal importance to the world. Why did he have to be so perfect for her? She would ask herself this whenever she thought of him, which was most days, and every night, which was something she would never admit to anyone.

"South America, how exciting," Catherine interjected, jarring Kimberly's wandering thoughts back to their conversation.

"What brings you back to California, Jake? Do you live here? Or are you here for an assignment and, if so, please share the sordid details with us. Hopefully, there are some!" Catherine teased.

"No sordid details, sorry." He grinned, and it emphasized the strong lines of his cheek bones and chin. "I live in New York, or should say, that is where I pay to keep my belongings stored, considering the amount of time I spend on the road," he answered with a brief smile and then continued in a more serious tone. "While I was in South America on a job assignment, Zane tracked me down. Our grandfather recently transferred to a rehab center to recuperate from a broken hip. I've taken a temporary leave of absence to be with him since Zane committed himself to an assignment in Asia for the next ten weeks. Until he's better, it looks as if I'm a resident of northern California again."

Jake shrugged and a grin curled the corner of his lips. "Once he finally agreed to move into a rehab center, Gramps insisted on returning to the San Francisco area. He claims that although his heart is in Texas, he wanted to be closer to at least one of his grandsons when he finally passes. We told him he'd be a long way off from dying if he would just do the physical therapy that the doctors prescribed. Unfortunately, he's more stubborn now at eighty-five than he was at sixty-five."

"I had no idea. I hope his recovery goes well. I always loved Grandpa Zack," Carly replied sincerely.

Kimberly returned her attention to the pasta on her plate. Despite the disheartening news about Jake's grandfather, she didn't miss the sparkle in her sister's eyes when Jake announced his plans to stay in California. Carly wanted to see she and Jake together, and that meant there would be no end to her sister's matchmaking schemes. If only she could figure out what went on in Carly's conniving mind, Kimberly might be able to prevent her heart and ego from any further damage.

She'd bet money, even now, that the longing she felt for him was written all over her face. More than anything, she wanted to curl up in a tight ball and cry when she thought about Jake's knowledge of her feelings for him. Why had she not realized it before now? Kimberly stared down at her plate and wondered how long it would be before Jake got bored and left them alone. "Thanks, Carly," he answered with a swift grin.

Kimberly glanced up and found that Jake's gaze had drifted back to her. She smiled politely at him despite the tremble that ricocheted over her skin in record time. He held her gaze and Kimberly squirmed under his intense scrutiny. He couldn't possibly know how one look from him caused her hands to tremble and her brain to turn to near mush.

"Jake?"

Kimberly breathed a sigh of relief when Jake released her gaze and turned his head toward Carly. "I'm sorry. What was that?"

"No problem, Jake," Carly replied slyly. "I asked where you're staying while in town? With Zane? Is he still living in Sausalito?"

"He is, but I'm in a hotel," he answered with a grimace. "Zane's out of the country until sometime in October, and he committed his place to some friends who are having their house remodeled, before he knew Gramps was coming back and that I would be taking a leave of absence to be with him. Zane's friends are staying at his place for the entire time he's gone. I dread the idea of living in an extended stay hotel for two or three months, so I'm going to check out Airbnb. Although, truthfully, I haven't gotten that far in my plans yet."

"What a coincidence, Jake!" Carly exclaimed and pushed herself to the edge of her chair. "Kimberly just told us about her plans to sublet a room in her house, maybe even on Airbnb!" she quickly added. "Kimberly has the cutest bungalow; she remodeled it herself. Wouldn't that be great, Jake? You could sort of be Kimberly's Airbnb-guinea-pig. You know, see if she really likes renting out a room or not?"

Kimberly popped her head up so quickly she was afraid she might have strained her neck muscles. "Carly, I don't think Jake would be interested in staying with me." Kimberly's gaze darted back and forth between Carly and Catherine, before finally landing on Jake. "I mean, I live in Sunnyvale. Your grandfather's rehabilitation center is probably in San Francisco or Sausalito, isn't it?"

"Actually, his rehab center is in Los Altos Hills," Jake replied.

"Oh," Kimberly replied, and she shot Carly a distinctive glare that she doubted Jake missed. He cracked a grin and Kimberly wasn't sure if she wanted to crawl under the table or run screaming into the house.

Jake leaned back in his chair, folded his arms in front of him, and his grin was still in place. "Thanks for the offer; this is great Kimberly. I'd like to move in tomorrow, if that works for you?"

She should have ran screaming into the house when she had the chance. "What?" Her head darted back and forth between Jake and Carly. "You, ah, my, a—"

"Really?" interrupted Carly. "This *is* great!" She turned toward Kimberly, her eyes wide, and her eyebrows arched to their highest heights. "You should go home right now and get the place ready. I'll come with you."

"Oh, boy." Catherine's gaze darted to Kimberly before she turned and glanced at Jake. To Kimberly's horror, Jake smiled back at Catherine, and she watched him return her friend's worried expression with a wink.

Jake unfolded his arms and rested his hands on his thighs. "Kimberly, I'm joking. I really do plan to check out some Airbnbs next week. Besides, I wouldn't impose myself on one of George's little sisters. I do have some redeeming qualities."

"Oh." Kimberly sucked in a deep breath and then quickly exhaled it. She looked away from Jake and Catherine right before she realized that she had dumped half a bottle of ketchup over her salad, instead of the burger on her plate. Why hadn't she ducked out of the party when she had the chance?

"Hey Jake! We're getting a game of football together, and we need another player. Still able to run old man?" George yelled from over the heads of a huddled group of guys gathered across the yard from them.

"I can, but can you?" Jake called in return. "Excuse me ladies, but I think I need to show a few guys how soft married life has made them."

Jake trotted away from their table without a backwards glance, and Kimberly was grateful because she was about to have one of the fiercest arguments that she'd ever had with her meddling sister.

Chapter 2

Jake circled the block for the third time before parking his car. The neighborhood was filled with people enjoying the day, many gardening or riding bikes on the warm summer afternoon. He glanced at the address contained within a text message, and a sigh escaped from his lips. He compared the address once again to the one on the mailbox, 642 Cobblestone Lane. He had the right address.

Once out of the car, he quickly scanned the area for any sign of the home's owner. He ran a swift hand through his hair and walked toward a set of wooden porch stairs. He'd lost his mind. He must have, or why else would he be doing something so reckless when he was well aware of the complications that would result because of it? He took several more steps, ignored the inner battle going on inside of him, and rapidly approached the screened door.

He surveyed his surroundings with hooded eyes. Flowerpots filled with California poppies sat on the porch, while bougainvillea hung from the roof's overhang. A pair of white wrought iron rocking chairs, adorned with brightly colored cushions, sat invitingly on the porch. The home was well taken care of by its owner. The two-story bungalow, with its peach and white stucco facade, promised peace and serenity. It was everything he was looking for and hadn't been able to find over the past week.

It had been only a few hours, although he had continued to look at places for several days, when he had grown tired of visiting the ultra-modern apartments he had found in his search on Airbnb. Many of the apartments, though tastefully decorated, gave off a sterile vibe. He would never be comfortable enough to relax, as he hoped to do during his time off. Worrying over something that spilled on the marble floor was not his idea of relaxation.

Besides, he openly admitted to himself for the first time in years, he was lonely. He longed for companionship, someone to share an occasional meal with or to watch a late-night movie. A roommate, if even for only a few weeks, would be a welcome change in his otherwise solitary life. Standing at the screen door, he reminded himself that a roommate, particularly this roommate, was strictly limited to a friends' only relationship. He needed no repeats of his life's past failures.

His gaze traveled over the screen door, and he noticed several pink hearts painted around the door knob. The corners of his mouth curved into a grin. The realization that he might have actually found the ideal place to stay for the next several weeks gave him the push he needed to ring the doorbell. So much for those few redeeming qualities he claimed to possess, he thought, and pressed the button for the second time.

"Coming," called the voice from inside the house, just as he had about decided that there wasn't anyone home. He shifted uncomfortably as he waited, pushing the tip of his boot at a piece of chipped wood on the porch floor.

"Hello?"

"Hi, Kimberly." Jake raised his sunglasses to the top of his head, taking with them the shoulder-length strands of hair framing his tanned face.

"Jake?" She stepped closer to the screen door. "My gosh, it is you. I'm sorry; I wasn't expecting you. I thought you were the FedEx man. I'm sorry, with those aviator glasses on and your hair down, I, ah, ah—"

"Please, don't apologize," he interrupted. "I'm here uninvited. As for my hair, I rarely wear it down and never on television. Far too radical for my producer to allow on his network. Did I interrupt you sunbathing or something?" Discreetly, or so he hoped, he admired her enticing figure, clad only in a bikini top and a pair of faded cut-off denim shorts. A very short pair, he couldn't help but notice, though he didn't want to. Kimberly Urbane, he reminded himself, was forbidden territory, and he needed to keep it that way for both of their sakes. Despite his own mental scolding, a bolt of desire seared through him, and he struggled to push the sensation aside.

"Oh, ah, no. I was out back, in the garden." A scarlet flush swept over her cheeks. "I was pulling weeds."

"Ah." He nodded toward her face. "That would explain the streak of dirt on your cheek."

"What?"

She rushed to rub her palm against her cheek, and he held up his hand to stop her. "I'm teasing Kimberly. No dirt. You're fine."

"Oh. Ah, okay. Please come in." She opened the screen door and directed him with a flutter of her hand toward the inside of the house.

"Thanks." Jake shut the door behind them, and he rubbed each of his palms, suddenly damp, against the soft denim of his jeans.

"Can I get you something to drink?"

Jake's gaze darted up to meet hers and he realized that she had caught him checking her out. "Ah...thanks, that would be great." Despite getting busted by her only moments earlier, he had to force himself to look away from her enticing backside and focus on the interior décor as he followed behind her. The living area was tastefully designed, with boldly colored accents against soft cream-colored furniture. The room vibe invited you in, and he found that he liked her style, a lot.

The clicking sound of his western-style boots against the ceramic tile echoed through the house as he followed her into the kitchen.

"Is lemonade okay?"

"Perfect." His gaze wandered over the white countertops and cabinets, again accented with vibrant accessories smartly placed throughout the kitchen. "Nice place. Carly said you are remodeling it yourself, didn't she?" He leaned his lower back against the side of the kitchen countertop and folded his arms across his chest. Unable to suppress his amusement, his grin widened as he watched her flutter around the kitchen, preparing their lemonade. He didn't want to make her nervous, he really didn't. Over time, once she had a chance to know him better, the more comfortable around him she would become and they could finally become friends. Hopefully, with any luck he could convince his libido to chill, and everything would be just fine between them.

He watched her bend down to pick up a large spoon she had dropped, and he ended up wiping a bead of sweat from his forehead. She had to be aware of the provocative picture she made; how could she not? And, with her looks and body, how could she possibly be nervous around him? She probably had men lined up at her door most days. Her black, curly hair lay in a long braid against her bare, slender back. The bikini top she wore, although conservative for California's standards, accentuated her full, rounded breasts, causing him to move his eyes to the kitchen window more than once.

"Thank you," he mumbled when Kimberly handed him a tall, chilled glass, the cold liquid a welcome reprieve from the heated sensations moving through his body. His emotions were running so unexpectedly hot that when Kimberly finally responded, it took him a few moments to understand that she had begun to answer his earlier question.

"Sort of, I guess. Much of the woodwork was already here; I just refinished it. George helped me put in a few closets upstairs, and I have to admit that I have applied more coats of stain than I ever dreamed I would in a lifetime."

"Impressive. You did a nice job."

She smiled at him, her full and generous lips tinted a soft pink, and he took another long, slow drink of lemonade.

"Thanks. I've lived here for almost six years, and I still find myself shocked by the work that needs to be done."

His gaze traveled to various sections of the kitchen and then returned to settle on her face. Her skin was smooth, with the briefest of freckles smattered across her nose, and he was tempted to reach out and run the pad of his thumb over them. He cleared his throat and dropped his hands to his sides before tucking each of them into a back pocket of his jeans. "You've done a good job. You must have moved in not long after graduating?"

"Yeah." She clasped her hands in front of her and then quickly released them to drop them at her sides. "I lived with my parents for a few years after college and then decided it was time to prove that I wasn't the shy, passive little thing everyone believed me to be."

Her eyebrow went up in a challenge for him to deny it, and he couldn't, because she was right; it was her friends' collective opinion of her. She was the observer rather than the center of attention. He sensed a silent strength within her that he found attractive, and it forced him to try even harder to maintain a distance between them. He could never take advantage of her feelings for him, and that's what he would be doing if they became involved, because it could never work out between them. Never. "Looks like you've done a pretty good job proving your point." He gestured with his hand to the cabinetry behind her.

"Thank you," she responded with a bright smile. "Just because I prefer to be behind a camera rather than in front of it, doesn't mean I was invisible like everyone seemed to treat me growing up."

He laughed. "I seem to recall you making yourself invisible several times when—"

"Yeah, well," she hastily interrupted. She placed a hand on each of her hips and tilted her head slightly to the side. "I've changed. I'll never have George's easy way with people or Carly's ability to command the attention of everyone in the room, but I've learned to hold my own. Which has me wondering, Jake." She paused and took a deep breath. "I'm not intentionally trying to sound rude or anything, but why are you here? And how did you get my address? Carly, I bet," she mumbled the answer to her own question loud enough for him to hear.

"Before you go blaming Carly, let me assure you, I reached out to her for it and not the other way around."

"Why?"

"Kim," he responded, realizing that he preferred the sound of her name in its shorter form as it rolled off his tongue. "Kim" sounded much more personal, he decided as an afterthought.

"I've visited over a dozen apartments in the last week. Each one I left more disappointed in than the one before it. I don't want to feel as if I'm living at a boutique hotel. I want to feel like I'm coming home at night. I want to be able to relax in the evenings." He paused, his brow furrowed in a frown.

"And?" she asked cautiously.

"And, I want to rent a room in your house." He exhaled a deep breath that was louder than he intended. He held up a hand when he thought she was about to protest. "Wait. Before you refuse, let me explain that I won't be around much during the day. I plan on visiting my grandfather every day, at least for a few hours, and there are a lot of friends I would like to see while I am back in town. Los Altos Hills is only ten minutes from here, so that makes your place convenient to Gramps' rehab center." He paused to watch the multitude of expressions cross her face, unable to gauge her reaction.

"I wouldn't expect you to cook, in fact, I'm rather a good cook myself, or at least I used to be, and I would be willing to make dinner every night," he told her. "I'm relatively neat. You wouldn't have to clean-up after me, and I'll do my fair share of chores. Please, Kimberly, I'm desperate. I know you weren't exactly thrilled when Carly originally suggested that I rent a room from you. I even teased you about it, but if you think about it, it really isn't that bad of an idea. For one, you wouldn't be taking in a stranger and two, the situation will only be temporary. I—" He stopped and set his drink down. "Kim, are you all right?"

She stopped choking long enough to reply, "Okay."

"Okay?" He pushed his lower back away from the counter and straightened. "Do you mean okay, as you're okay and can breathe? Or okay, as in I can move in, okay?"

"Okay, as in you can move in okay," she responded between coughs. "As for breathing, I'm not sure about that yet. Lemonade went down the wrong way."

"Are you serious?"

She looked straight at him, and her dark eyes were glistening with merriment. "Not about the breathing. But, yes, you can move in." The corner of her lips twisted upward and, in a voice still rough from the bout of coughing, she replied, "you had me at willing to make dinner every night."

If he hadn't lectured himself throughout the day about keeping their relationship platonic, Jake would have reached out and kissed her. He had been prepared to provide her with an ample amount of begging, perhaps even throw in the offer of grocery shopping, which was something he definitely didn't enjoy but was prepared to do, if it sealed the deal with her. The corners of Jake's mouth tilted upward. "I did? You mean I could have skipped the part about chores?"

"Nice try. I plan to hold you to the cooking and the chores. You can count on it."

He chuckled and assumed she would live up to her word. "Kim, I can't thank you enough. I don't have much stuff, a couple suitcases full of clothes and... is that a dog barking?"

Kimberly whipped around to look out of the large kitchen window at the back of the room. "Whoops! I left Daisy in the backyard. She probably heard us talking and thinks she's missing out on something. I'll be right back," she called over her shoulder as she rushed out the back door of the kitchen.

He became conscious of his gaze eagerly following her departure out of the back door and reminded himself of the *do not trespass* sign he planned to visualize each time he was tempted to look at her. He swallowed hard and instead tried to visualize her dog. "Daisy?" He repeated and chuckled. The image of a Shiatsu with red painted nails and a bow on top of its head formed in his mind, despite the deep barking sounds coming from the backyard.

Kimberly returned to the kitchen with her dog, and he unconsciously took a step backward. "That's

Daisy?" He tried to keep his mouth from gaping open and failed. He watched the large St. Bernard bask in its beautiful owner's attention and realized he shouldn't have been surprised by her choice of canines. Besides her initial nervousness this afternoon, everything he had witnessed so far today, including her choice in pets, proved Kimberly Urbane was not as timid or reserved as most people believed.

"Isn't she adorable?" Kimberly laughed happily as the dog planted several sloppy kisses on her face. "I found her roaming the streets two years ago. Her fur was matted, and she appeared not to have eaten in a while. After numerous calls to the police department failed to turn up anything, I posted lost and found posters throughout the neighborhood. The vet checked for a chip, and she didn't have one. I also posted to several lost dogs' sites. When I didn't receive feedback from anyone, I declared Daisy officially mine. The vet thinks she's about three years old. I assumed that whoever owned her probably couldn't keep her anymore because of her size."

She tilted her head to look up at him. "You're not allergic to dogs, are you?" she asked, and Jake wondered if she secretly hoped he was, so she could escape from what she would eventually realize was a very hasty decision on her part.

"Allergic? No. I just wasn't expecting a St. Bernard, I guess." Kim appeared so carefree and happy, even with the dog slopping all over her, that it nearly took his breath away. He silently cursed. He needed to put a halt to any wayward thoughts about her, or staying at her place would be out of the question. She might provide him with killer smiles, and wear shorts that left him in a near pant, but she did not give off vibes that implied a willingness to flutter in and out of a sexual relationship. Although she might be independent and much stronger than people believed, she still had a vulnerable innocence about her that flashed large red lights before his eyes. Nope, she would never accept a casual affair with him, and a casual affair was all he was willing to offer her, to offer any woman, ever. Kimberly Urbane was not for him, and he was going to make sure it stayed that way while living in her house. He might need to remind himself of it daily, he conceded, if his sweaty palms meant anything besides a reaction to the warm summer day.

"I'd like to move in this weekend, if that's okay?" Jake asked and deliberately pushed his wandering thoughts aside.

"Sure," she responded hesitantly.

Jake was not reassured by the tone of her voice nor the way she clung to Daisy as if her life depended on it. "Are you sure?"

"No, it's fine."

"You're sure?"

She nodded. "I am," she answered and smiled at him.

"All right then, I'll need a key."

"No problem. I have a spare, but I'll have another one made at the hardware store this week."

"Will it be all right for me to park in the driveway?"

She stared back at him, her eyes sparkling in the brightly lit kitchen. "You can park in the garage, if you'd like? I only have the one car, so there's always an extra space. It's probably safer, anyway. I'd hate for some thieves to think the house's contents are as nice as the Ferrari sitting in the driveway," she added with a hint of laughter in her voice.

A smirk creased the corner of his mouth. "California is one of those places where you can rent about anything you want on a whim, if you have the money." He surprised himself with his inexplicable need to explain that the two-hundred and fifty-thousand-dollar car parked in front of her house was a frivolous impulse while he was in California and not an example of his current values.

"Except apartments," she responded coyly, her full, generous lips twitching in amusement. Her dark eyes continued to sparkle as she looked up at him, and once again, he noticed that she really had grown up into a remarkably attractive woman, inside and out.

"Except apartments," he returned, joining in on her amusement with a deep chuckle of his own. God, she was beautiful when she laughed. Hell, when wasn't she beautiful? His eyes roamed, for the last time he promised himself, over her long legs and slightly rounded hips snugly covered in a pair of shorts that should be sold with a label that read 'illegal if worn in public.'

He coughed and shook away a piece of hair that fell into his face. The breeze that recently ruffled the kitchen curtains must have suddenly stopped, because his internal body temperature skyrocketed, and his skin was sticky. He took a large gulp of air and admitted to himself that the temperature of the kitchen had nothing to do with the reason his jeans suddenly fit tighter, particularly in one noticeable area. "I better get going. I want to see my grandfather this afternoon." He shifted back and forth by pressing his heels into the floor. He was eager to put some space between Kimberly's scantily clad body, and his overly aroused one, in order to hide his reaction to her.

"Ah, okay."

He didn't miss the curiosity peppering her simple reply, but there was no way he planned to explain his sudden need to leave, not a chance. Discreetly as possible under the circumstances, he pulled at his jeans to loosen the fabric.

They walked together to the front of the house, and Jake opened the front door.

"I'll see you Saturday." He stepped out into the bright sunlight and placed his sunglasses over his eyes. He flashed her a smile and then proceeded down the stairs and toward his car.

*****

"See you Saturday," Kimberly murmured as she watched Jake make his way to the flashy red sports car. As soon as she was positive that he had driven away and didn't appear to be coming back, she decided that she didn't have the luxury to dwell on his hasty departure. With a grimace on her lips, she raced up the stairs to the second floor, Daisy following close on her heels.

"Two days! How will I ever get this room ready in two days?" She moved a large cardboard box filled with pictures from the seat of a folding chair and slumped down in defeat. Her guestroom was a disaster, having been used as her junk room until now. Never needing it for anything other than storage, she had left it last on her list to remodel, never having found the time to do it.

"Why I ever thought I would have room in a three-bedroom house is beyond me." Kimberly occupied one bedroom herself and had turned another into a home office. She had allowed the third bedroom to morph into a convenient storage room, and now she regretted it.

She moaned out loud, her eyes roaming over the dozens of photographs she had taken over the last few years, proudly framed, but never hung. Her eyes wavered briefly on the many cardboard boxes scattered all over the room, containing everything from high school yearbooks to childhood dolls. She refused to dwell on the many pieces of fitness equipment set up in the room, purchased as various New Year's resolutions yet never used.

Somewhere under all the clutter was a double bed that would need to have the linen changed and the quilt aired out. Forcing herself to look at the room's brightly papered walls almost caused her to cry. Large yellow daffodils stared back at her distressed expression. She cringed as she realized that the wallpaper must have been put up in the seventies, definitely one of the country's gaudier eras.

"Well, Daisy," she directed at the large, panting dog at her feet, "so much for our walk in the park this afternoon. It looks as if I'm off to the hardware store for some supplies." The shaggy dog merely gave her a blank stare before returning to rest her head on her huge, outstretched paws. She gave out a low growl and closed her eyes.

"Sure, take a nap, why don't you? Meanwhile, I have to empty out this room, tear off all the wallpaper, and then paint it when I'm done." She let out a long sigh and then allowed a grin to spread slowly across her lips. "But you know what, Daisy? It's going to be worth it." She glanced at the St. Bernard, now snoring loudly, and shook her head. She had spent nearly twenty years in love with Jake Taylor without ever doing anything about it, and the last week feeling sorry for herself because he knew of her feelings but never returned them. What made matters worse, he had always been nice to her. If he had been a jerk, she might have given up on him long ago. She leaned back in the chair and stared up at the ceiling. Maybe Carly was right. Maybe the timing had never been right for the two of them and now was her chance?

Jake would be living under her roof, possibly for several weeks, and she could finally to go after her dreams. Her decision to rent a room to him might have been a split second one, but it was a good one. She had caught him checking her out more than once today, and he had been interested, if only in her body, and for now that was better than nothing. This was the chance for him to see her as something other than George Urbane's little sister, and she was going to make sure he did. Jake Taylor was going to realize that he loved her as much as she loved him. She didn't have the details worked out yet, but she would. This was her chance with him, and she planned to take full advantage of it.

She stood up and then retreated to her bedroom to change into clothing suitable for the hardware store. "Carly," she giggled to herself, "this idea of yours better work. Not that I will give you credit, little sister, if it does."

Chapter 3

Kimberly yawned for the fourth time in a matter of minutes, desperate to wipe away the fatigue from her eyes. Although one of her favorite songs blared from the speakers in her bedroom across the hallway, the loud, pounding music was not doing a good job of keeping her energized. She was exhausted. She had spent the past twelve hours scrubbing off layers of wallpaper and then patching the drywall that had come off with it.

Despite all her efforts of the last two days, she had a long way to go if she planned to have Jake's room ready by morning. She needed to finish painting the room and then give the walls time to dry. Jake expected to move in the following day, and it was bad enough she would have to explain the pungent smell of paint throughout the house.

She opened the second can of paint and poured some of it into a pan. She had just placed the roller brush into the paint when she heard the doorbell ring. "Now who could that be?" She grumbled with a glance at the old clock radio sitting in the middle of the floor. "At eight o'clock on a Friday night? Really?"

Kimberly walked down the stairs, wiping her hands on the front of her denim overalls as she did. She glanced through the window at the side of the front door and had to do a double take. "Jake?" A bolt of panic ran through her at full force.

She inhaled a deep breath and opened the door. "What are you doing here?" She ran a shaky hand over her wild black curls, pulled together with a band at the back of her head.

"I hope I'm not interrupting anything?" He stuck a hand into his front pocket and stared back at her, golden speckles highlighting the dark orbs of his eyes. "I went to visit my grandfather and, well, I drove by and saw the lights on. I thought you might want to go out and grab something to eat?"

"Ah, gee, I would love to, but not tonight, Jake. I, ah, am sort of busy, thanks anyway." She glanced back at him with a look that, she hoped, would convince him to leave. She brushed a piece of wandering hair that had escaped from her ponytail and slid to the side of her cheek, and he continued to watch her. She stiffened her spine as she held the door open only wide enough for her to stand between it and the door frame. Why wouldn't he take the hint she gave him and leave? Not only did she need to finish painting the bedroom, she looked as if she hadn't bathed in a week, which wasn't the truth, although the timing of her last shower was foggy to her sleep-deprived mind. Seeing him in a pair of low riding jeans and neatly pressed Lacrosse shirt that matched the color of his eyes made her glance at her own pair of grungy overalls, splattered with God only knew what. She glanced up and found him staring at the top of her head.

"What's in your hair, Kimberly? Is that paste?" He stretched his hand through the narrow door opening and pulled a thick clump of grayish muck off of a long black lock.

"I give up. Just come in." She opened the door wide enough for him to enter through it. Unable to stop herself, she released an exaggerated sigh before ushering him into the foyer. She wanted to comment on his ungracious assumption that she was alone this evening, but she was too tired to bother, and besides, her disheveled appearance had to make that obvious to him.

"What in the world are you doing?" he asked, amusement dancing in his eyes. She grimaced as he cocked a dark eyebrow in her direction after openly assessing her appearance.

"Well, if you must know, I've been painting your damn bedroom," she answered more harshly than she intended. Embarrassment, combined with her present exhaustion, had her at her wits' end.

"You're what?" he replied in complete disbelief.

Kimberly tucked a stand of hair behind her ear. "Please, Jake, I'm in no mood to explain. All I want right now is something to drink and to sit down. How about a beer?" Though not much of a drinker, she kept a six-pack of Stella in the refrigerator for guests that sounded inviting at the moment.

"Sure." He paused to stare sharply into her eyes before he followed her into the kitchen.

"Now, you want to explain to me what you meant by painting my room?" He reached for the beer she held out to him, his eyes hard and unrelenting.

Kimberly squirmed under his scrutiny but refused to respond.

"Kim, you had no intention of subletting a room to me or anyone else, did you? Carly made the whole thing up. Am I right?"

Kimberly stared mutely into her bottle of beer, too tired to make up an excuse in either her sister's or her own defense.

Jake sat down across from her at the small kitchen table, and she squirmed in her seat as he searched her face. He leaned over and nudged her chin up tenderly with his thumb and then shook his head. "Why didn't you tell me when I was here the other day, Kimberly? Why didn't you tell me that Carly had made

34

up the whole thing?" He tilted his head slightly to the side and looked at her, the expression in his eyes puzzled.

"I, you, you needed a place to stay," she told him. It's also my opportunity for you to finally notice me, to fall in love with me, she silently added. Although, if she looked as bad as she thought she did, her plan had already backfired on her. "I, it's, okay. I look much worse than I feel. A shower and some sleep should keep me from scaring you tomorrow." She laughed nervously.

Jake's firm mouth curved slightly upward at the corners before he released her chin from his grasp. He leaned back against the chair, his arms crossed over his chest, his eyes still locked on her.

Kimberly straightened. "Is, ah, everything okay?"

He considered her for a moment, his amber eyes focused on her face. He blinked several times and then he shook his head. "I've been on my own for a long time." He stopped to stare at a random space on the floor. "I'm not used to someone doing something nice for me, who wasn't paid to do it."

He raised his eyes and returned her gaze with a hooded expression. "Zane and I see each other on the rare holiday, and, well, Gramps is there for me but he's almost eighty-six years old and not doing well." His eyes softened, became less intense, and he uncrossed his arms. He wiped the palm of each hand down a pant leg and then smiled back at her. "I'm sorry, I'm rambling."

"Jake, it's okay, I wanted—"

"Kim," he interrupted. "Whatever your reasons, I'm grateful. I really am desperate for a place to stay, and you helped me when you didn't have to. However," he began with a threatening arch of a thick eyebrow, "while I'm staying here, any work that needs to be done, particularly something like painting my room, will be done by me. I will not sit on the couch watching television while you fix up the house, so forget it. And don't even say it. I'm a chauvinist, and I know it. Consider it a way of satisfying my insatiable male ego, but I will do the house repairs."

"Jake," she began with a renewed vigor, grateful for the turn of events in her favor. He planned stay, he wasn't angry with her for her small fib, and he had volunteered to do house repairs. Things were turning out better than she could have imagined, but she certainly didn't have to let him know it, not yet. "I have been living on my own for six years and have done just fine, thank you very much. Anything I need done, I will do myself," she finished with a triumphant gleam in her eye, hoping he would take the bait as her brother had done so many times in similar situations. She might as well kill two birds with one stone, she thought, and struggled to hold back a smile. She'd get free work, which meant Jake and she would spend more time together, and hopefully, with any luck, and perhaps a bikini or two, he would fall in love with her in the process.

"This is not negotiable Kim, so don't even go there with me." He pulled his cellphone from the front pocket of his jeans. "Tonight, there are only two things left for you to do before you are off to bed, and that is to get some food in you and to take a hot shower. So, while you are doing that, I will order us a pizza. Then, little Miss I-Can- Do- It- Myself, I will finish painting my room." He bent his head over his phone and tapped several times on the screen.

"Jake, but I can't—"

He raised his head, the look in his eyes playful but the set of his jaw determined. "No buts about it. Now march up those stairs and into the shower while I order the pizza. Go!"

Kimberly stood up. "Fine. The truth is, I don't care if I ever see another paint brush again." And she hoped she didn't, because all she wanted was to stand under the hot shower and never come out.

Jake set his phone down on the table and stood up. She caught site of his rakish grin, and it shot through her like an arrow to her heart.

He reached out to her, placed a hand on each of her shoulders, turned her around, and gently pushed her toward the stairs. "Good, because the only thing you need to do right now is take a long, hot shower."

"Okay, okay. If you insist, but I'm warning you Jake Taylor, I will not be bullied," she called over her shoulder as she ran up the stairs, a mischievous smile curving her lips.

****

"I could smell the pizza from my bedroom," Kimberly exclaimed as she stepped out of the hallway and into the guest bedroom. She stopped in mid-step to take in the sight of Jake standing on a stepladder, his bare back facing her. She ran the tip of her tongue over her dry lips as she realized he must have removed his shirt to avoid getting paint on it. Her eyes glazed over, mesmerized by the strong muscles in his back contracting and relaxing with each stroke of the paintbrush. She couldn't help but admire the way his jeans hung low and inviting on his narrow hips.

The thought of him turning around and facing her with his broad, naked chest terrified and excited her at the same time. She swallowed hard. Her entire body was suddenly melting inside. She hoped he'd assume that the flush crawling over her skin was because of the hot shower she had recently vacated and not her wayward lust showing its true colors.

"The box is over in the corner. I want to finish the last of this trim. Eat," he told her without turning around. He continued to paint while she headed for the pizza.

"It smells wonderful," she commented. She kneeled on the floor next to their dinner and pushed a hunk of her damp, black hair laying loose in a mass of curls, to the back of her shoulder. She sighed appreciatively as she opened the large pizza box.

"I hope you like mushrooms and green peppers?" He stepped off of the step stool and placed the paintbrush down on top of the paint can. After wiping his hands on a rag, he joined her on the floor.

"Nice pajamas," he remarked with a nod at her baggy sweatpants and extra-large Stanford T-shirt.

She swallowed a bite of pizza and smiled at him. "I typically wear a black leather teddy to bed, but unfortunately it's at the dry cleaners."

Jake's hand paused in mid-air, the slice of pizza never making it to his mouth. "Really?"

She tilted her head slightly to the side. Her brows arched high on her forehead, and her eyes followed them. "You are such a typical guy. And the answer is, no. I live with a St. Bernard, Jake. I doubt Daisy would be impressed with a teddy. Besides, I prefer comfort over style," she responded defensively, crossing her legs in front of her.

She took a bite of her pizza and swallowed. "Let me guess. You're one of those men who wears silk pajamas to bed? I'm right, aren't I?" she teased playfully. She was determined to keep her eyes focused on his face, refusing to allow her attention to wander to his chest, despite her desire to check-out every exposed inch of his muscle laden torso.

"Actually, I don't wear any... let's just say, I don't wear silk pajamas," he hastily amended.

He set what was left of his slice of pizza, down on the box. "Kim." He released an exaggerated breath. "I guess this is as good as time as any to discuss this." He paused and took a drink from his beer before placing the empty bottle down on the floor. He ran a swift hand over the hair confined at his nape, and he stared down at his half-eaten pizza. "Since my divorce, women haven't exactly been on the top of my priority list. Not that I don't like them anymore..." His head darted up, and he looked straight into her dark eyes and softly chuckled.

She watched him struggle to explain. She wondered about it, her lips twitching with possibilities. "Ah, okay."

"What I'm trying to say is that you don't have to worry about me bringing women here. I wouldn't do that to you. I respect the fact that I'm a guest in your house, but that's not to say if you, ah, you know. I mean, I never stopped to think before that maybe, perhaps, I'm invading your privacy? I want you to know if you have someone, you know, staying overnight." He coughed uneasily. "You can tell me to go and get lost. I can get a hotel room, or...what the hell is so funny?" He paused, and his eyebrows narrowed over his eyes. He was obviously irritated because she found humor in what was an awkward conversation for him. A warm thrilled cursed through her.

"You." She laughed and quickly placed her bottle of beer down on the floor. "Jake." She rubbed her palm down the leg of her sweatpants. "I'm sorry, and you tried to be so serious, too. It's just that I'm at home painting your room on a Friday night. I'm not an expert, but I would have to assume that's not a great example of an active love life." She straightened her back, and her expression became serious. "I guess, what *I'm* trying to say is that I don't have much of a social life either, particularly in the area of overnight guests. Not that I'd object.... I mean, ah..." The words tumbled out before she had a chance to stop them. Hurriedly, she reached for their empty beer bottles before uncrossing her legs and standing up.

"Why don't we drown our dull lives in another beer?" she suggested with an inquiring tilt of her brows toward the bottles.

Jake smiled at her, and she was reminded of why she found him so irresistible. His lips, while not overly generous, were a pale rust color, and when they curved into a grin, and they often did, she wanted to reach out and trace them with her fingertips.

"Sounds good, although I can't guarantee what the walls will look like after I've had a few beers," he answered. He stood up, stretching to his full height.

Fascinated by the sight of him raising his arms above his head in a lazy sigh, Kimberly found herself unable to watch him without wanting to drool. He closed his eyes, which gave her the opportunity to study him without his knowledge. His chest was covered in a soft golden matte of hair that gradually tapered into a V down his torso, until it disappeared into the waistband of his jeans. She wanted nothing more than to trace the outline of each finely defined muscle in his taut stomach with her fingernails. She raised her eyes and found him returning her gaze with an amused expression in his eyes. She quickly looked away. "I, ah, will be right back," she stammered before fleeing the room.

It wasn't until she was safely in the kitchen that she was able to breathe normally again. If ever a man could be described as beautiful, it was Jake Taylor. A jolt of longing coursed through her, and she brought her fist to her mouth. Before she knew it, she found herself leaning against the refrigerator door for support because her knees had gone weak. "Get control of yourself," she whispered under her breath. "Jake is here for a short time, and it is not because of you. At least not until you figure out how to change his mind otherwise, which, by the way, Kimberly Urbane, you suck at." She opened the refrigerator door and reached inside for two bottles of beer.

A quick glance out the kitchen window reminded her to check on Daisy. "Daisy?" she called out the back door. "There you are, girl. How are you doing, sweetie?" She walked out to the back porch and then sat on the edge of a wicker chair. Daisy took the opportunity to jump up and slather a series of sloppy kisses across her face, and Kimberly felt some of her earlier anxiety disappear.

"I know you want to come in, but not while we are painting. I read online that you could get sick if you lick any paint, which we both know is something you would try to do, so you're staying outside for a little while longer. Yes, I know, Daisy, I'll miss you too," she crooned, amused by the dog's attempt to sit on her lap.

She gave Daisy one last pat on her shaggy head before returning indoors. Kimberly was grateful for the warm night air and that Daisy could stay outside and out of trouble. She sighed, if only she could do the same thing.

Jake was waiting for the drink she offered to get him, and she couldn't stay in the kitchen avoiding him forever. She grabbed a beer with each hand and left the room. Remember, you want him to get to know you, so stop staring at him like you want to jump his bones. Just don't look at his bare chest, and you'll be all right, she silently repeated as she climbed the stairs. Or his muscular arms, she mentally added with another step. Or his sinewy back, or his chiseled cheekbones, or.... "I am in so much trouble," she whispered anxiously before entering the room.

"Did you run out to the grocery store for more beer?"

He put the paintbrush down, wiped his hands on a rag, and then reached for the beer she handed out to him. "Thanks." Jake twisted off the cap and took a long, slow drink from the bottle. Kimberly watched him, mouth gaping, until she realized what she had done and quickly returned to her seat on the floor. She anxiously moistened her lips with the tip of her tongue.

"Thanks." She looked up at him and a playful grin creased his lips before he turned away and reached for the paintbrush again. "I went out back to check on Daisy." She placed her beer beside her, reached for one of the few remaining boxes of photos in the room, and then placed it on her lap. She had to get in control of her emotions and not make them so obvious around him. She was not a silly girl with a crush on him; she was a strong, independent woman who loved him. She needed to show him the difference, and so far, despite her admittedly weak attempts, all she had done was drool over him. She sucked in a deep breath and reached inside of the box.

"I hope Miss Daisy isn't too upset because we're inside eating pizza, while she's forced to stay outside?"

"Ha, no, she's fine."

He painted for several more minutes before he remarked, "By the way, where did the name Daisy come from? Kind of unexpected for a two-hundred-pound St. Bernard. You mentioned that she didn't have any tags. I assume you named her?"

"It was simple." She looked up from the photographs she had been sorting to gaze back at him. Once again, she found herself staring at his backside and did not complain one bit about it. Low rider jeans really were one of the world's greatest inventions. She ran her tongue over her lips and forced herself to hold back a sigh of longing. "Growing up, the only true animal lovers in my family were my grandmother and me. Grandma always had at least a few stray animals living with her, dogs, cats, even a pig for a while." She paused and put a photo in a pile with several others. "Once I knew I planned to keep the big fur ball and had to think of a name of a name for her, I instantly thought of my grandmother."

"And your grandmother's name was Daisy?"

"Of course not." She giggled, unable to stop herself. "My grandmother's name was Lily. Daisies were her favorite flower. A St. Bernard named Lily would sound ridiculous, Jake."

Jake twisted his upper body from his place on the step ladder to look down at her. "Kim." His deep, rich voice was peppered with laughter. "You have a very witty sense of humor."

She smiled back at him, pleased by his compliment, and returned her attention to the stack of photos.

"Does your grandmother live in the Bay area?" he asked after a few minutes of silence.

She looked up from a photograph of Daisy that she had taken a few days after she had found her and smiled longingly. "Actually, she died five years ago."

"I'm sorry, Kim. I didn't know."

"It's okay." She paused to flip through several more photographs. "I have little things, or should I say big things, like Daisy to remind me of her."

"You're fortunate." His hand stopped in mid-air, the paintbrush never quite reaching the wall. He stepped off of the ladder and laid the paintbrush down on the can. He reached for his beer and took a long drink.

Jake set his beer bottle on the bottom step of the foot stool. He secured the lid on the paint can and gathered together the dirty brushes and rollers. "I think that's it for tonight. I'll be able to determine in the morning whether the walls need another coat or not."

"Wow." Her eyes darted around the room. "I was so caught up in sorting photos, I didn't realize you had made so much progress. The room looks great, Jake. Thanks."

"No, thank you, Kim. I'll wash the paint brushes, and then I'm heading to my hotel. I don't know about you, but I'm exhausted."

"Forget the brushes; I'll wash them out. I really appreciate your help." Her smile quickly faded as she watched him stretch his T-shirt over his head. His stomach muscles contracted in response to the movement, emphasizing the sharply defined muscles under his deeply tanned skin. She took a large gulp of air, jumped up from her seat on the floor, and scurried out of the room like a frightened mouse before he caught her drooling over him again. If Jake wondered where she'd gone, he'd figure it out soon enough when he found her waiting at the front door for him.

"I'll be going to see my grandfather in the morning, so I should be here around two o'clock tomorrow. It will still be early enough in the day in case I need put on a second coat of paint." He opened the front door and breathed in the warm California night air.

"Jake," she said before he had the chance to say goodnight. "I wondered. I mean, I thought perhaps, if it was okay, that I might go with you when you see your grandfather sometime? I didn't know him as well as Carly did, but he used to come to our house for dinner occasionally, and I thought it might be nice to see him. If it's okay with you?"

Jake studied her upturned face for a brief moment, and she had to force herself not to squirm under his intense scrutiny. "Sure." He smiled faintly. "Maybe next week?"

She smiled softly in return. "See you tomorrow."

"Goodnight." He looked at her, and with a quick wink, he turned and walked away.

Once again, Kimberly found herself following his movements until he reached his car and drove away. She shut the door and locked it. She made her way through the kitchen and opened the backdoor to let Daisy inside.

She doubted that she had made any progress in her effort to win Jake's love tonight; he certainly didn't give her any positive vibes if she had. Her disheveled appearance likely didn't help, although she had caught him watching her a few times tonight. Or was he returning her stare? She shook her head. Didn't matter, she wasn't giving up on him. She was determined not to get discouraged. A tiny smile curved her lips. She might need every minute of his stay to convince him that she was the one for him, but she was up for the challenge. She yearned for Jake Taylor to return her love and planned to do whatever it took to make that happen. In the meantime, she would hold him to his earlier offer. Jake claimed that he wanted to be responsible for the work around the house, and she'd let him. She mentally wrote a list of home repair projects she needed completed while she turned off the lights and made her way up the stairs and into bed. Her lips continued to tilt upward until they grew into a large smile.

Chapter 4

Kimberly looked into the tiny mirror attached to the passenger side visor and visibly winced. "Your grandfather is going to think that I look like a witch," she exclaimed as she attempted to smooth the mass of curls that, fifteen minutes ago, had lain in soft waves against her shoulders.

"You should have told me, Kim. We could have rolled up the windows and turned on the air conditioning." He pulled the Ferrari into a visitor's parking spot at the rehabilitation center with a swift turn of the steering wheel. He turned the ignition off, released his seatbelt, and then turned to face her. He took a strand of tangled curls between his fingers, rubbing the silky hair between his thumb and forefinger. "I wouldn't say a witch exactly, Kim. Marge Simpson maybe, but not a witch." He looked straight into her eyes, his gaze burning her with its intensity.

She managed a tremulous smile in return. "Thanks a lot." She choked out a laugh while she tried to get a grip on her emotions. She reached out to pull her hair from his grasp and paused. She looked up to find his eyes had gone serious, the previous teasing that caused them to sparkle no longer evident.

He moved his head toward her with the slightest of movements.

"Jake?"

He blinked and released her hair, slipping his hand from underneath hers. He swiftly turned away and grabbed the car keys. "We better go inside. My grandfather is expecting me."

Kimberly nodded although she didn't understand what had just happened or, more specifically, what hadn't happened. He had wanted to kiss her. She knew he had. She saw the desire in his eyes just as she was sure he witnessed the same in her own. Confused and needing some air, she reached for the door handle with shaking hands and bolted from the confinement of the sports car.

Her heart hammered in her chest as she waited for Jake to get out of the Ferrari. Every self-help blog she subscribed to would tell her to confront him, to make the move he was hesitant to make, but she couldn't, not yet, especially since this was the first time that he had shown any interest in her other than friendship. She didn't want to make the wrong move or push him before he was ready, when clearly, he wasn't.

She had decided the morning before he moved in, after a sleepless night, that she wasn't going to create any grand plan to make him fall in love with her. Instead, she would be herself around him and let the chips fall where they may. Either he fell in love with her, or he didn't. She never believed in playing emotional head games, and she didn't plan to start now.

Since he had moved in a week ago, they had spent part of each day together. Her work load was light, and she had time on her hands, as did Jake, leaving them both with plenty of time to spend in each other's company. They took turns making dinner and then shared it on the back patio, relaxing in the lawn chairs after making small talk. They went for walks with Daisy and stayed up late watching movies. Not once had he made any type of gesture toward her that she could consider anything but strictly platonic, and it killed her. She found herself reluctant to go to bed at night and eager to wake up in the morning, cherishing every moment they spent together, and she had no idea whether he felt the same way or not.

He only had to look at her with those golden eyes of his, and she wanted to fall into his arms. She had to keep reminding herself to be patient, regardless of how it tortured her to do so. She wanted him to fall in love with her, not use her as a convenient bedmate while in town. Jake traveled all over the world, and beautiful women likely threw themselves at him every opportunity they received, and she didn't want to get placed in the same category. Besides, she undoubtedly paled in comparison to the glamorous and experienced women he was accustomed to, the type of woman she never wanted to be. She loved spending time in her garden or taking photographs in the park. She preferred a quiet dinner at home rather than a meal at some trendy restaurant, and she began to think Jake did too. He didn't talk much about himself, but he appeared happy in her company and relaxed when they were together. She leaned her back against the car while she waited for him, taking a deep breath in an attempt to get her emotions under control.

*****

Jake remained in the car, his dark brows drawn together. He pressed his eyes shut. He had been holding a strand of her hair between his fingers when the urge to kiss her had overcome him. He hadn't realized he had moved toward her until he heard her whisper his name. Fortunately, he realized what he had done, or more precisely, shouldn't be doing, before it was too late. Even though the desire to taste those red, heart-shaped lips had crossed his mind a hundred times over the last week, he couldn't let it happen.

If tasting her lips was the only thing he thought about when he was with her, he might not be worried. His mind went into a direction of its own every time he so much as glanced at her. Looking out the car window, he shook his head in hopes of clearing the arousing images of Kimberly that kept forming in his mind. They had to remain friends. He genuinely felt comfortable with her, and it had been a long time, if ever, that he had felt that way with a woman. He couldn't take advantage of the feelings she tried to hide from him, and he couldn't allow any of his own to gain control of his heart. A relationship that was anything more than friends would end in disaster; there was no other outcome for them. He'd already seen this movie and held a starring role in it, and it hadn't ended well for anyone. He couldn't do that to Kimberly, and he most definitely couldn't live with the guilt that came with hurting her in the process.

Ignoring her questioning look when he finally got out of the car, Jake directed her towards the large brick building in front of them with a nod of his head.

"I have to warn you." He paused to open the large glass door for her. "My grandfather's state of mind is unpredictable these days. Sometimes he is as ornery as ever, and other days, it's like he's depressed. One day last week, he didn't even wake up while I was here. I don't know if it's the medication, or his broken hip and the therapy it has required him to do, but he definitely has good days and bad days. I'm telling you this, so you won't be disappointed if he is not in the best of moods or even sleeps through our visit." He started to place his hand on the small of her back and realized that touching her would be a mistake, particularly since the yellow sundress she wore glided over her like a glove and had him itching to touch her. Instead, he directed her down the white hallway of the rehabilitation center with a swift motion of his hand.

"I understand, Jake, I do."

He had asked her over breakfast this morning if she wanted to go with him, and she had been thrilled with the invitation. She told him that the large, boisterous Texan that used to join her parents for drinks or dinner had awed her as an adolescent. The stories she shared with him brought back memories of his own, and he was reminded of how fortunate he was to have the old man in his life... and how alone he would be when that was no longer the case.

He mentally braced himself as he opened the door to his grandfather's room.

"Gramps, you awake?"

"Perfect timing, Mr. Taylor. Your grandfather just finished taking his medicine. Haven't you, Zachary?" The nurse practically yelled in order to be heard over the booming voices coming from the television. Waiting for a reply that never came, the nurse finally shook her head. "He's all yours." She sent Jake a knowing smile. "Good luck, he's in full temper today."

"Thanks," Jake mouthed to the nurse before she left the room. He gave Kimberly a tentative smile before walking over to his grandfather's bedside. His grandfather lay propped up with several pillows behind his head and back, his gaze trained on the corner of the room.

"Gramps, it's me. Jake. Your grandson."

"For cryin' out loud, boy. I know who you are. I raised you from a boy, didn't I? And don't be talkin' slow as if I've lost my senses, either," grumbled the old man.

"Gramps, why didn't you say anything when I walked in?"

"Because it's two o'clock, and between you and that confounded nurse, I haven't been able to hear one word of my television program. Only doggone show worth watching, and ain't no one here who lets me watch it in peace. That one there," he pointed to the television with a wrinkled hand as a rugged, handsome soap opera star appeared on the screen. "Reminds me of myself years ago, that one does. He's from Houston, you know, his brother too. Damn fools they are, always have some woman distracting them from taking over the state's largest oil company. Wife has a split personality too, a damn shame."

Jake glanced at Kimberly, not surprised to see her puzzled expression. A smirk crept up on his lips. "He overheard one of the nurses talking about how surprised they were to see some TV drama that took place in Texas back on television. That was all Gramps needed to hear. He's been hooked ever since," He shifted his gaze to find his grandfather ignoring him again, as the old man's attention returned to the television blaring from the corner of the room.

He glanced at Kimberly, and she smiled back at him. Her gaze returned to his grandfather, and it went soft. He assumed she was trying to adjust to the sight of his thick crop of hair, once a rich black, now predominately white, and his large frame now withered to a shadow of himself.

"Should we come back later?" she whispered with a soft giggle.

"No way." Jake shook his head determinedly. "It's John Wayne marathon week, starting at three-thirty. He won't even talk to us then, will you, Gramps?"

"I give up, Jake. Turn the blasted contraption off. And who is us?" he asked, finally moving his attention from the television to look at his grandson.

Kimberly reached out and placed her hand on the side of the bed rail. "It's Kimberly. Kimberly Urbane, Mr. Taylor. I grew up down the street from you in Los Altos

Hills." A wide smile creased her lips. Her eyes sparkled with merriment when she glanced at Jake, and he responded with a grateful wink. "Thought you had straw-colored hair?" the rough, old Texan rasped with narrowed eyes.

"That's Carly, my younger sister."

"Ah, yes. She was a rascal, that one," he responded with a chuckle. His eyes widened with recollection. "Now I remember you. You're the little mouse who would hide on the stairs when I would visit your parents. Thought you would probably run away and join a convent when you got the chance," he stated with another deep chuckle.

Kimberly pulled her lower lip between her teeth. "Nope, no convent for me. Actually, I'm a photographer." Kimberly shot a glance in Jake's direction.

"Another one who can't keep a steady job either, I reckon," he replied with a meaningful glance at his grandson.

Jake was unable to hold back the sudden cough that erupted from deep inside him. He glimpsed at Kimberly and found her lips twitching, glad that she had a hard time keeping a straight face also.

"Gramps doesn't consider my job as a reporter honest work. You don't work with the soil or get your hands dirty working in television. He obviously feels the same way about photographers."

His grandfather raised his hand and pointed a wrinkled finger at him. "And you don't go wearin' your hair in no ponytail, either. You weren't brought up that way. It must be that dang job of yours, allowing you to keep that hair of yours long like you do. At least you finally have a woman who believes in looking like one," he grumbled with a glance of appreciation toward Kimberly. "If my grandson here gives you a rough time, you holler. I'll take care of him."

"Thank you, I will."

Jake glanced up and found her cheeks tinged with pink. He longed to run his fingers along the smooth skin, to trace each curve of her face.

"He can be a wild one, that's for sure, just like his brother, Zane," his grandfather said, breaking into his wandering thoughts. "I'm glad to see Jake's finally got the common sense to settle down and give me some great-grandchildren—"

"Gramps," Jake hastily interrupted. His focus returned to his grandfather where he should have left it, if he had any common sense at all, which, apparently, he didn't. "I forgot to bring you some chocolate. Kim, do you mind running down to the cafeteria and getting a candy bar for him? Gramps has a terrible sweet tooth, which I try to appease with some cookies or a candy bar." He reached into his wallet and grabbed several dollar bills from it.

"I don't want no choc—"

"Here." Jake reached over and thrust the money into Kimberly's hand. "The cafeteria is on the second floor. Thanks, Kim."

"Ah, sure, I'll be back in a few minutes." Kimberly gave him a confused look in response to his silent plea. Even so, to his relief, she reached out and closed her hand around the money.

Jake watched her close the door behind her before he returned his attention to his grandfather. "Gramps, I need you to understand that Kimberly came with me today to visit you, not because she plans to have your great-grandchildren with me. That is not only ridiculous, but it's also impossible."

A loud growl emitted from the old man's lips. "Now, don't go talkin' no hogwash with me, boy. My old body may be confined in this bed here, but that doesn't mean I lost control of my senses. How many times have I told you that those over-paid city doctors don't know what they're talking about? All that mumbo jumbo about you having the mumps and not being able to have kids. If we had been living in Texas, we would have seen a specialist who knew what they were talking about. Biggest mistake I ever made was when I listened to that quack doctor in California. That, and trusting your mother to have an ounce of sense in her head," he grumbled with a sigh of resignation.

"Gramps, we've been over this a million times. I had a severe case of mumps as a teenager. I can't have children because of it, and I've learned to accept it... No, let me finish—" he softly demanded when his grandfather tried to interrupt. "I can't have kids Gramps, and I spent three hellish years with Brenda proving it. I won't go through that again, ever," he vowed more harshly than he intended. Reigning in his sea of emotions, he finished in a softer tone, "Kimberly is a wonderful person, and I'm sure she wants to have a family of her own someday. I can't give that to her, and she deserves nothing less. Please Gramps, don't bring it up again."

He ran his fingers through his hair. A tremble in his hand that wasn't there minutes ago was now visible. "For whatever reason, Kimberly likes you, and I know she will want to visit again. She's a sensitive person, Gramps, and I don't want to see her get hurt by your senseless rattling."

His grandfather let out a large, exaggerated breath. "Dag-blast it, Jake...all right, but that doesn't mean I agree with you," he muttered obstinately as a yawn escaped from his thin lips.

"Thanks, Gramps."

"Those blasted pills the nurse forced down my throat have done tuckered me out, boy. Otherwise, I'd wear your ear out arguing." The old man's voice was groggy with sleep.

Jake reached out and took the older man's weathered hand in his own and gently squeezed it. He watched his grandfather's eyes flutter shut. He was worn out. He tired so easily these days, which Jake acknowledged with a heavy heart. When Kimberly returned, they would leave Gramps to rest. Jake reached out and brushed away a stray piece of hair from the old man's forehead, watching the gentle rise and fall of his chest. Jake wondered how he could be expected to go on without his grandfather always being there for him. No matter where he was in the world, he knew he had his grandfather to go home to, and soon that would no longer be the case. Jake swallowed back the anguished lump welling up in his throat when the door opened.

"I hope he likes Hershey bars?" Kimberly held up a bar in each hand.

"Thanks." Jake nodded his head toward his grandfather's still form. "He's asleep. He dozes off rather quickly now. You can leave the candy bars on the table for him."

Kimberly placed the chocolate on the bedtable and then followed Jake out of the room. They walked down the empty hallway in silence.

"Thank you for bringing me," she murmured once they settled in the car and she secured her seatbelt.

"He enjoyed seeing you, Kim." Jake started the engine but hesitated before shifting the car into reverse. He stared out the front windshield for several seconds before turning to look at her.

"Look." He paused and took a deep breath. "I hope you'll ignore anything my grandfather said today. He, well, took my divorce rather hard. Maybe harder than I did," he noted with a brief grunt. "Not that he cared much for Brenda, because he didn't. He thought

55

she was a high class, uppity bit...never mind. Anyway, he's convinced that I'm unhappy being alone. And, ah, when I brought you here today, he got the wrong impression."

She turned her head and provided him a smile that did not reach her eyes. "Jake, it was an easy thing to misconstrue. I understand perfectly." She turned her gaze to the outside of the car.

"Good." He straightened his shoulders and placed the car in reverse. "And you don't have to worry about it happening again, because I set my grandfather straight. I told him there was nothing between us and that we're strictly friends."

"Great," she responded softly. She rolled down the window, tilted her head toward the outside of the car, and allowed the cool breeze to whip across her face.

From the corner of his eye, Jake spied her eyes squeezed shut and her shoulders slumped.
"Yeah...great," he repeated without enthusiasm. Damn, Gramps, he thought, and a surge of pain rushed through him. It can't work between Kimberly and me. It can't.

Chapter 5

Kimberly slowly opened the front door, trying hard, but quickly failing, to avoid making noise while she entered the house. She immediately heard a squeaking sound and cursed under her breath for not oiling the door hinges as she had always meant to. It was one o'clock in the morning, and the loud creaking sound was bound to wake up Daisy, who in turn, would wake up Jake. She locked the door behind her and proceeded to tiptoe to the hall closet to hang up her jacket. "So far so good," she whispered with mixed emotions. While it was a relief that Daisy hadn't discovered her entrance yet, she did question the two-hundred-pound St. Bernard's abilities as a watchdog.

She placed her purse down on a table in the hallway and decided to get a glass of water for herself before going to bed. She yawned leisurely as she crept along the hallway, feeling her way in the dark. If she turned on even one light, she was sure to wake up Daisy, who was probably snoring away upstairs, sprawled across Kimberly's bed.

She entered the kitchen and walked directly to the sink without turning on the light. She opened the cabinet door and reached inside for a glass. She had one hand on the door handle and the other clasped around a glass when a wisp of warm air spread across the back of her neck.

"Where have you been?"

"Jake!" She dropped the glass from her hand before she could stop herself. She watched the glass clamber against the counter top and then roll into the sink, relieved when it didn't break. "You scared me half to death!" She turned around to face him and found herself within inches of being in his embrace, a place she had dreamed about during the last several weeks.

Her eyes widened in surprise to see the deep concern emanating from his hazel eyes.

"Then we're even." He released a sigh, and it echoed through the kitchen.

Kimberly twisted her hands together at her waist. "I, ah—"

"Do you realize," he interrupted in barely a whisper, "that I have paced this damn house wondering where the hell you have been? I've been out of my mind for the last several hours with possibilities, and none of them good." The worry in his voice came across to her loud and clear.

"Jake, I'm sorry," she stammered. She inched herself backward, pressing the small of her back against the lower kitchen cabinets. Just because she didn't understand why he was so upset didn't mean she needed to provoke him any further, and she suspected the reek of wine wouldn't help. One of the models had tripped tonight, and the contents of her glass went flying across the room to land on Kimberly's blouse. Fortunately, the wine was white; unfortunately, she now smelled like a wine bar.

Despite all her efforts to place some distance between them, they remained less than a few inches apart. "I, ah, we finished the photo shoot earlier than expected, two days in fact. Everyone working on the catalog, you know, the other photographers and models, went out to celebrate. I couldn't exactly refuse. I had worked just as hard as everyone else, and I deserved to celebrate also." She stared back at him with a defiant lift of her chin.

"I'm not saying you didn't work hard or that you don't deserve to celebrate your efforts." He paused to push a strand of hair behind his ear. "I'm saying that I was worried. For the last three weeks, you've only come home once past six o'clock. Even then, you called to let me know you would be an hour late. Tonight, you're seven hours late, and I don't hear a word from you. I called you no less than three times and sent you a text—"

"I said I'm sorry, Jake," she interjected. "What more do you want me to say? I would have responded, but my phone battery died, and I forgot my charger. Heather, one of the models, invited us to an impromptu party out in the Bay on her yacht. Before I knew it, it was after midnight, and the party broke up. I came straight home."

"I suppose I should be grateful for that ingenious thought; otherwise I may have waited up for you all night." He planted a hand on each of his hips and continued to watch her with narrowed eyes and tightly clenched jaw.

"Jake. I said I'm sorry twice now. I promise, I won't do it again. However, I *am* a grown woman, and you sound just like my father." She knew that when she had time to think about his reaction, his concern would thrill her, but she was exhausted and wanted only to go to bed. She had been up at the crack of dawn, out the door, and at the studio by six a.m., preparing for another twelve-hour day, followed by the wrap up party.

Kimberly dared to look him in the eyes, and the heat of his gaze burned right through her. The clouds must have shifted, because she noticed that the moonlight now beamed through the kitchen window, casting a glow over the kitchen, and emphasizing the disappointment reflected in his eyes and etched on his face. She had screwed up tonight, and Jake's expression confirmed it. Her behavior was nothing above that of someone who was selfish and self-centered.

"That's what Carly said," he mumbled.

"What did you say?" Her eyes grew wide, and she clenched her hands into small fists at her sides.

"I, ah, called your sister tonight—"

"You what?" she screeched, her voice echoing throughout the kitchen.

"Kim, I had no idea where you were, and I was worried," he defended. "It was getting late, and I thought you may have stopped by Carly's. Maybe it was one of your niece's birthdays or something, and you thought you had mentioned it to me? I don't know." He ran his fingers swiftly through his hair. He shifted uncomfortably, his eyes staring over her head at the wall, and she assumed it was to avoid her blazing glare.

Her mouth gaped open as she stared back at him. "I can't believe you called Carly," she groaned out loud, and her shoulders slumped. "My life as I know it is over, Jake." She covered her face with her hands as she shook her head in disbelief.

"I realize that calling Carly this evening wasn't the brightest idea I've ever laid claim to, but you are sisters. Don't you speak to each other regularly? Don't sisters visit each other or drop in unexpectedly? Obviously not," he muttered. "Nor do they inform family members of their current houseguests."

She dropped her hands to her sides and raised her head up to look at him. "What?"

"Carly was surprised to learn that I had been staying with you, Kim. Why is that?" he asked, the irritation in his voice ringing loud and clear in her ears.

"Jake," she began in an exasperated voice, "Carly is an incurable matchmaker. She's bound to, no, she will definitely read far more into your staying here than there is. Not to mention, she'll blabber it to anyone who will listen and then take credit for it." Silently, she added, even worse, she will blame me when you move out without a backward glance in my direction. Her life was officially a disaster. Jake was mad at her, and Carly was probably posting invites for her and Jake's couple shower on Facebook, but Kimberly couldn't even get him to think of her as more than a friend. All she did was go out for one night with co-workers; that's it. Just one lousy night.

She glanced at Jake, and to her surprise, his expression transformed from one of disappointment to one of... could it be... desire? Her lips parted, and a jolt of awareness shot over her skin like scalding water. The irritation she had seen in his eyes and that had pulsed from the clenching of his jaw was replaced with an expression she'd only noticed once on his face, and that was the first time she had visited his grandfather with him. Could the intensity reflected in eyes actually be desire? She took a quick, shallow breath.

Jake took a step forward. "Would that really be so bad?" He bent his head precariously close to hers. He rose a challenging eyebrow, daring her to respond.

"That Carly would blabber and take credit?" she stammered, her smile awkward in her nervousness. She stared at the wall behind his shoulder, afraid that if she looked into his eyes again, she would discover something other than desire staring back at her, and she wanted to dream for just a few more moments.

Jake stood a few inches from her. One small step, and she would practically be in his arms, her breasts pressed snugly against his chest. She felt her pulse quickening as she yearned to run her hands through his hair, now loose and tucked behind his ears, the tips of the golden strands brushing against his shoulders. Hesitantly, she turned her head and looked in his eyes, and she discovered the desire was still there, glowing from his eyes. She swallowed anxiously. What was going on with him? One minute, he looked at her with disappointment, and the next, he undressed her with his eyes. A tremble coursed along her spine, and her lips slowly parted.

"I was referring to something going on between us, Kim."

It took only mere seconds before he lowered his head to hers, pressing his warm, caressing lips against her own. His large hands encircled her waist, bringing her flush against his hard body. Gradually, he coaxed her mouth open, his tongue eager in its exploration, and she responded with equal enthusiasm. His hands traveled over her back, eventually gliding across her breasts. Her nipples hardened with desire, and she pressed them against the palms of his hands.

A deep moan escaped from her as she moved further into his embrace. The evidence of his arousal pressed against her pelvis, and waves of desire spiraled through her. While his lips continued to devour her, his hands glided upward, burying themselves in her hair. Slowly, his lips left hers to explore the skin on her neck, and she groaned out loud.

Her heart pounded, and a tremble coursed through her. Hesitantly, her hands roamed over his broad shoulders, then upward, combing through his tawny strands of hair. She ran her nails along the back of his neck, delighting in his growl of pleasure. He felt good, so good.

He eased his hands out of her hair and slid them once again across her breasts, where they lingered only for a moment before reaching her waist. With one swift motion, he lifted her up and set her on top of the kitchen counter. Her eyes widened, but she held on tight with her hands clasped behind his neck. Moving his body quickly between her legs, any questions she had about his intentions were answered when he pulled the tail of her blouse from her jeans.

One by one, he unbuttoned her blouse with deft fingers until it gaped open. He bent his head to her waist, his lips following hotly in the path of his hands. His hands caressed the skin on her back as his tongue slid sensuously across her stomach and rib bones. Her breath came in shallow gasps as he snapped open the front of her lacy bra.

He lifted his head and gazed at her with eyes laced heavily with passion, and she smiled, hoping to reassure him that he required no further approval for his actions. He returned her smile with a wicked one of his own before he bent his head and took one rosy peak between his lips. He sucked wildly, his tongue moving back and forth over the aroused tip as his hips moved in a slow, rhythmic motion against the apex of her thighs. She wanted him inside her more than she had every wanted anything else in her life.

Kimberly's breath came out in ragged pants, as the onslaught of his lips on her breast drove her nearly over the edge. She braced her hands on the top of the counter for support, arching herself closer to him. She circled her long, jean-clad legs around his back, and his throbbing arousal ground into her. She was on fire, her entire being ready to burst into flames.

Jake released her swollen nipple from his lips, and she panted in anticipation of where his mouth might travel next. His tongue traced her collarbone and neck with a series of hot circular motions before finding her mouth once again. She parted her lips gladly. His lips continued to torment her as he picked her off the counter and slid her down his hard body. Gently, he slid her blouse off, and allowed it to cascade to the floor, at their feet.

He lowered his mouth to ravish her other breast with equal care, his hands making haste with the buttons of her jeans, when a distinctive scratching noise filtered throughout the kitchen.

"Damn," he swore under his breath.

"Mmm, what is it?" Kimberly asked, her eyes glazed with a film of desire.

"Daisy." His breath was rapid and coming out in gasps.

"Daisy?" She blinked her eyes and wondered why the name sounded familiar. "Oh no, Daisy!" she exclaimed when the distinctive scratching sound suddenly combined with a full-fledged bark. She opened her eyes, and looked at Jake. The fog of desire that had clouded his eyes earlier was gone. "I forgot all about her."

Jake's lip parted to form a wistful grin. "I let her out back right before you came home because she had been whining to go out. I take it that she is ready to come in," he added with a disgusted shake of his head. He removed his hands from their resting spot on her hips and let them drop to his sides.

He shook his golden hair from his eyes as he reached down for her blouse, laying puddled at their feet. "Ah, here, you better put this on."

"Jake, I, ah, we..." She reached for her blouse from his outstretched hand. The heat he had stirred within in her had faded away, and a tremble traveled over her skin.

"Don't say it, Kim. Let's leave it be. Please. Daisy obviously has a lot more common sense than we do and impeccable timing, I might add," he finished with a ragged sigh.

She stared at him. His eyes were downcast and focused on a spot on the floor behind her. She wanted to argue with him, but his expression indicated that any questions she had for him would not be answered tonight. "I think I'll go to my room now, if you will take care of Daisy?"

*****

Jake nodded and then watched her walk away. He was unable to take his eyes off of her as she hastily swept out of the kitchen.

He ran the palm of hand across his mouth and chin while the dog continued to bark. No longer able to allow himself to stand in the middle of the kitchen in a stupor, he walked toward the backdoor and opened it.

"I'm coming, you damned dog," he hissed under his breath, and immediately a sense of guilt washed over him for placing the blame on Daisy for his overactive libido. The panting dog pounced into the house the second he opened the back door. Taking care to remember the mud she normally tracked in from the backyard, Jake grabbed a rag and rubbed down her feet.

"Daisy, girl. You sure know how to take care of your mistress, don't you?" He placed his hand on her back and absently rubbed the fur on her back until she began to squirm. Regret filling him, he lifted one of the dog's back paws for cleaning. He reached for one of her front paws, and Daisy bent her head and licked his face. Jake chuckled although, deep inside, his heart ached.

"Well, don't worry, girl. It won't happen again. My emotions ran rather high tonight. I was worried...okay and slightly angry," he amended when Daisy turned her shaggy head in his direction, cocking, what he swore, was a shaggy eyebrow at him.

"Give me a break, will you, dog? I worried about her all evening and then, when I try to do something about it, I find out her family doesn't even know I'm living at her house. I mean, come on, Daisy. What's the

65

big deal? We're grown adults." Daisy growled playfully and then plopped down on the braided rug in the middle of the floor.

"Okay, I get your drift. I've sworn off marriage, love, and anything remotely associated to them. And nothing will change my mind." He tossed the dirty rag into a basket by the back door.

Daisy lifted her head, a low growl escaped her large, salivating mouth.

"What? Can't two people occasionally enjoy themselves without walking down the aisle?"

The large St. Bernard growled louder.

Jake ran a hand through the hair at the side of his head. "Okay, okay. I get it, Daisy. No wonder you don't have any interested suitors sniffing around here. You are too old-fashioned for most of the dogs in the neighborhood." He looked down at her and laughed because it occurred to him that he had been trying to hold a conversation with a St. Bernard. Man, he had definitely lost it. He ran his hand across his stubble-covered chin, and then sure he would never sleep, he decided to have the drink he had needed all evening.

As he approached the small liquor cabinet in the corner of the family room, he wondered what had come over him. In his mind, he saw Kimberly walk into the kitchen and open the cabinet door. Obviously, he had not been lost enough in his concern for her to miss the chance to admire her enticing bottom snugly poured into a pair of tight jeans or to notice her thick, rich mane of hair cascading down her back and its distinctive honey scent filling his senses.

The smell of wine trailed in her wake and increased his irritation. She had been out enjoying herself, while he sat home alone waiting for her. "Alone," he repeated out loud. Was that his problem? He mixed himself a drink from the bar and tried to make sense of his behavior tonight. For nearly a month, he had had little to look forward to other than Kimberly's return from work. He had spent several hours visiting his Grandfather each day, coupled with the few home improvement projects that he volunteered to do around the house, but mostly he was alone.

It was ironic, he decided with a startling realization, because he spent a considerable time alone as an international journalist and it had never bothered him before. He lived for months in foreign countries with no one closer to him than the other journalists and photographers whom he met on assignments. Yet, now he spent his time, regardless of what he had been doing, longing to see Kim each night.

Jake took a large swig from his glass, disturbed by this latest revelation. He needed to put a stop to his obsession with her. He planned to return to New York as soon as his brother came home and could stand vigil over their grandfather, and no one, not even a 5' 10", raven-haired beauty, could stop him. He placed his glass down on an end table and walked over to the built-in sound system. He pulled up his playlist on his cellphone and chose a song from Hozier. The artist's music seemed to match his mood perfectly.

He reached for his drink and settled down on the couch with Daisy snoring softly at his feet. He had been a fool to start something with Kim tonight and could only be grateful it had ended when it had. A crushing weight of despair bore down on him. It had felt so good, so right to hold her in his arms, tasting each delectable inch of her. God, how he wanted to bury himself into her velvety warmth and stay there forever. "Forever, what a joke." He leaned back against the couch with an air of defeat engulfing him. He drank deeply from his glass and swiftly emptied its contents before he returned the glass to its place on the end table. There was no forever for him and definitely not with Kimberly Urbane.

Kimberly, he learned after flipping through hundreds of photographs housed in the dozens of albums she kept scattered throughout the house, loved children. At least half of her photos contained a child with their tiny faces smiling happily at the camera. He had asked her about the photos over dinner one day last week, and she had explained that she began her career as a local photographer, her specialty being children because she loved to capture the happiness and open trust in their small faces. The photo albums were portfolios of her work. When she could no longer pass up the lure of a steady paycheck and the health insurance that came with it, she had traded in the photography work she did locally with friends for a position with the magazine.

Jake stared blankly out the window, oblivious to the moonlight that shone down on him. His thoughts drifted to his disastrous marriage. In the stillness of the room, he could hear years of Brenda's vile accusations being flung at him. "If you wanted children, Jake, you would take the tests. But you won't, because you really don't want children, do you? Do you?" she screamed. The hate-filled memories ran rapidly through his mind.

"I want children," he whispered hoarsely. He bent his head in sorrow, cradling it between his hands. After ten years, almost twenty if he counted the time from the doctor's prognosis his sophomore year in high school, he finally released all the pain he had kept locked up inside of him, the pain that had been slowly building, patiently waiting to be unleashed.

Alone, and in a room illuminated only by the moon, Jake wept for all the years he had spent without love. But mostly, he shed tears for all the years he would yet have to endure without the love of a woman like

Kimberly and the love of children he could never have with her. He wiped the palm of his hand across his eyelids. Tonight had been a reality check and a reminder for him. He had carelessly, and selfishly, taunted Kimberly with the possibility of a relationship that was more than platonic, and he would make sure it never happened again.

Chapter 6

Kimberly walked down the stairs with slow, methodical steps. Her hair, still damp from her shower, was pulled tightly into a braid that kept falling over the front of her right shoulder. Her white running shoes made soft taps on the tile floor as she approached the kitchen with less than eager steps. She had been mentally preparing herself for this moment for over two hours. Actually, she wearily admitted to herself, it was more like seven if she considered the hours she had spent staring at her bedroom ceiling until dawn.

As she neared the kitchen, she heard the clinking sound of metal hitting ceramic. Jake was definitely awake and in the kitchen, most likely eating his daily bowl of cereal. She took a deep breath upon entering the room, trying desperately to calm her inner trembling. "Good morning."

Jake glanced up from the newspaper he had spread out on the kitchen table. "Good morning." He glanced up at her, and the heat of his gaze went straight to her heart. Just as quickly, he returned his attention to the newspaper, and her spirits plummeted.

"There's still plenty of coffee left," he commented without looking up again.

"Thanks," she mumbled with a forced brightness. She walked over to the refrigerator while avoiding a glance in the direction of the sink area. She didn't think she could ever look at the kitchen counter again without being reminded of last night. A flush burned its way up her neck and rested upon her cheekbones as she tried to erase the intimate scene she and Jake had created on that piece of white quartz.

She pressed her eyes closed as the events of the previous night flashed through her mind for the thousandth time. She tried to push away the feel of his fingers slowly, erotically, unbuttoning her blouse to let it fall carelessly at their feet, while he aroused her as no other man had ever come close to doing. She shook her head and opened her eyes. A shiver crawled over her skin as she opened the cabinet and reached inside for a coffee cup. Even hours later, she could feel the warmth of Jake's breath on her neck, which caused her insides to go weak. She clenched the ceramic mug in her hand, desperate in her desire to force the erotic sensations from her mind.

She poured herself a cup of coffee with shaking hands. Relax, her conscience scolded. If Jake prefers to act as if nothing transpired between the two of you last night, that's okay. He just needed time to come to terms with his feelings for her, that's all, she mentally argued. Who cares if you laid awake until the sun first peeked over the horizon, your body aching with unfulfilled desire? Or that a mere glimpse of his mouth reminds you of his gentle, moist lips caressing you into an impassioned frenzy?

"Stop it."

"What's that?" Jake asked as he turned another page of the newspaper.

"What? Oh, nothing." She brought the coffee cup to her mouth and sipped from it. The shrilling sound of her cellphone echoed through the kitchen, and she practically flew across the kitchen to grab it from its charger.

"Hello?" She listened patiently to the caller for several seconds before she replied.

"Why no, Linda, I haven't forgotten about George's birthday party. I'll definitely be there." She walked across the kitchen to the refrigerator with the cellphone cradled between her ear and shoulder and looked out the window. "Yes, of course. I will make sure to bring my camera so that we'll be able to capture George's surprise on film." She watched Daisy chase a rabbit across the yard, relieved when the small creature escaped under the fence into the yard next door.

"Jake?" she repeated and caught her cellphone right before it fell out of her hand. "Why, um, yes, he's staying here." Reluctantly, she glanced at him. Jake's head shot up from the newspaper at the sound of his name and he arched a dark, questioning eyebrow in her direction.

"Well, I don't know if he's available, Linda. I guess you would have to ask him," she suggested with a smirk in his direction. "Except he's not in," she amended, in response to the pleading gesture he shot her.

Jake let out a large sigh of relief when he heard her next words, and she wanted to tell him that he owed her, but she bit her tongue instead. "Sure, I'll give him the message. Thanks for calling, Linda. I'll see you on Saturday."

"Thanks," he replied once she disconnected the call, relief evident in his voice.

"Don't be too grateful; you're not completely off the hook. Linda called to invite us to George's thirty-fifth birthday party at the Oaks Country Club this Saturday night. I told her that while I would be there, you would have to let her know." She sat down at the kitchen table, her earlier uneasiness now replaced with thoughts of her sister and her big mouth.

"Apparently, Linda called Catherine, who was on the other line with Carly, who mentioned your present residence. *I would have felt just terrible if Jake had been staying with you, and I failed to invite him to George's party,*" she mimicked in her best imitation of Linda's sweet drawl. Even though she loved her sister-in-law, her thoughtfulness tended to get on her nerves, particularly when they extended to inviting Jake to George's birthday party.

Jake winced before standing up and pushing his chair away from the table. "Oh. I, ah, better get going. Gramps is expecting me, and I've yet to go out for a run this morning." He placed the cereal box back in the cabinet and then rinsed his dishes off in the sink. "Any plans for today?" he asked. He opened the dishwasher and placed his bowl and spoon inside.

"None other than a day spent at the park with Daisy," she answered and took a sip of her coffee, her head buried in the front page of the newspaper. She intentionally mimicked his earlier behavior, aware that it was childish on her part, but she didn't care. She was hurt, and he deserved to know it.

"Then I guess I'll see you later."

"Okay," she responded distractedly, determined to keep her voice as uninterested as possible. She waited anxiously for the sound of the front door to close before she dropped her head to the table and onto her folded arms.

"How could he act as if nothing happened last night?" she cried out with a pound of her fist onto the tabletop. He was as cool as a cucumber this morning, while she was forced to hide her visibly shaking hands underneath the kitchen table. "Men." She clenched her teeth together. If she said anything to him about last night, he might accuse her of being suffocating, and if she didn't, he might think last night didn't matter to her. What to do next was the million-dollar question of the day.

She stood up and placed her empty coffee mug in the sink. She needed a distraction and decided that a day in the park, with her camera and Daisy in tow, was actually the ideal solution.

****

Jake entered the park and within minutes, he spotted Kimberly's red and black checkered blanket sprawled out on the grass near the pond's edge. As he approached the spot she had chosen for her day's outing, he noticed it was littered with the remnants of a half-eaten lunch. A camera bag, an empty Butternut Bread package, and dog biscuits also laid scattered across the blanket. "She has to be around here somewhere," he murmured. He raised his hand to shade his eyes, hoping as he did to find her amongst the park's many visitors.

When his initial search failed to find her, and unable to believe Kimberly would leave her belongings unattended for any length of time, he scanned the park area for a second time. His eyes darted across the short width of the pond to the opposite side from where he sat on top of her blanket.

He found her.

A familiar pain settled in the pit of his stomach as he watched her. Although they had been living together for over a month, he was still amazed by his reaction each time he saw her. The once shy, black-haired kitten, as he thought of her as a child, had transformed into a mysteriously exotic feline. A tightening formed in the region of his chest, near his heart, as he watched her brush her long braid back over her shoulder. She squatted near the water's edge with her camera in hand. She should be the one being photographed, not a flock of ducks.

He recalled the one glimpse of her this morning that he had dared to take, when she was on the phone with her back turned to him. He felt his blood pressure rise in response to the mental image that formed in his mind. As if a pair of black cotton yoga shorts that molded themselves to her narrow hips and tightly rounded buttocks wasn't enough to drive him over the edge of insanity, a UCLA T-shirt that ended at her midriff and exposed nearly all the creamy skin on her stomach had forced him to make a hasty retreat from the kitchen. He had lied this morning, for lack of a better excuse, to leave the house. He had been up and out for a run in the predawn hours because thoughts of her caused sleep to elude him. The torture he had inflicted upon himself with an additional five miles this morning was well deserved, although neither run had cleared the prior evening's events, or the desire that had come with them, from his mind.

He watched Kimberly toss several pieces of bread to the squawking ducks with one hand, as she snapped pictures with the other. He could tell, despite the distance, that she had little success in getting the ducks to come within less than a few yards of her. He chuckled as he tried to figure out why she would think the ducks would come anywhere near her with Daisy seated beside her.

He imagined her trying to explain to the ducks, in a soothing voice no less, that the salivating beast at her side was harmless and that she and Daisy were simply there to take their picture. He laughed again and decided that he could watch her forever. Damn, there was that word again. "Forever. Why does it keep coming up when I am trying so hard to push it away?" he asked himself in a tormented breath. The continual torture he put himself through, day after day, had to stop, and he had proved it last night with her. He had lost all control the moment his lips had brushed against her skin, and if Daisy hadn't interrupted when she did, well, he didn't want to think about the remorse he would be feeling today. He needed to place some distance between them, and yet, he found himself unable to do it. Even with the best of efforts, he couldn't convince himself that it was simply a coincidence that they were at the park at the same time this afternoon.

He hadn't even fooled his grandfather this morning into believing his thoughts were anywhere but with Kimberly. Grandpa Zack had sensed his eagerness to be somewhere else five minutes after he walked through the door. Gramps had repeatedly asked where Kimberly was, blaming the questions on his old age and failing memory, rather than his sly perception and knowledge of his grandson.

Jake watched her in the distance, and the memory of her soft, welcoming lips eagerly returning his kisses the previous night taunted him. He rubbed his palms together and was reminded of the warmth of her silky skin beneath his rough, callused hands. He never imagined finding a woman whose body felt so right against his, her feminine curves fitting perfectly against him.

He had to stop thinking about her. Each day he spent with her, he felt himself falling deeper under the mystical spell she wove around him; each time, she came closer to taking ownership of his heart. If only he were more like his brother, Zane, and able to leave his emotions out of a relationship. A love them and leave them kind of guy: that was his brother.

Years ago, baffled by his brother's ability to walk away from some of the most beautiful and interesting women Jake had ever met, he had asked Zane, after one of his brother's many broken affairs, how he did it. Giving him with a rakish grin that Jake was sure was part of his appeal, Zane had confided, ever so eloquently, that love stinks. In Zane's opinion, it was better to get going while the going was good, or you would find yourself with a broken heart and a pile of credit card bills.

Kimberly stood up and stretched her long limbs, and Jake ached with frustration. He decided with a renewed determination that Zane couldn't be more right. Jake needed to be moving on and soon, as love did, indeed, stink. A smile creased his tanned face, until moments later when he felt his lips freeze in place and his heart beat rapidly in his chest. He wiped his palms on his thighs as he took a deep gulp of air. *Love? Love stinks?* No. He couldn't be in love with Kimberly. Lust, sure, but love, no. He knew better. Love, no way, it was not for him. He was not in love with Kimberly.

He ran his hand through his wind-swept hair, determined to return home before the cause of all his reckless emotions spotted him. He looked up and then swore under his breath, as he caught sight of Kimberly waving at him. She was halfway around the small pond, Daisy trotting happily behind her.

"Jake, what are you doing here?" she asked hesitantly when she approached him. She gracefully folded her long, slender legs under her, and she sat down next to him on the blanket.

"I was out for a walk and saw your stuff. I thought I'd say hello."

She retrieved two bottles of water from her cooler and held one out to him. She took a sip of water and then smiled back at him.

Jake gladly accepted the bottle, eager for the cold water to cool off his conflicting emotions. "Thanks." He took a long drink of water, glad for the distraction it provided him.

She sipped from the bottle of water as her gaze wandered to the sky. "Beautiful, isn't it?" Her gaze was dreamy, her chestnut eyes following the path of an eagle soaring overhead.

"Yes," he replied truthfully, unable to tear his eyes away from her.

Kimberly gazed back at him with a puzzled look in her eyes. "I thought you already went for a run today?"

Two actually, he mentally replied. "I did. However, after visiting my grandfather today and making a few phone calls when I returned home, I found myself with some free time. I decided to take a walk to the park."

"Oh."

"I spoke to Zane."

"Really? Where is he, anyway?" She rested her hand on Daisy's back, absently petting the dog lying at her side.

"The Philippines. He and his team are returning home soon. His plans are to be back in the Bay area by the end of October," he paused momentarily before continuing, his gaze wandering over to the pond. "Who would ever believe Zane Taylor would become a plastic surgeon, treating children with severe challenges? Amazing, isn't it?"

Kimberly rested her hands on her lap. "I don't know, Jake. You forget that Zane was only a year ahead of me in school, and from what I recall, he was only too eager to play doctor with my friends and me."

Jake laughed. She was more than kind with her description of his brother's sexual prowess. "That's Zane for you. He always loved a pretty girl."

"I don't think love is the word I'd use, Jake," she added with a wide grin.

Jake swallowed the last of his water, grateful to not have choked on the cold drink. "No, I guess you're right." He chuckled and placed the empty bottle inside her cooler.

"I've decided to give up my apartment in New York." His gaze remained focused on the pond off in the distance. He placed his hand on Daisy's head and ruffled her hair, while he looked out over the water.

"Really? Why is that?"

He dared to glance into her eyes and saw the hope radiating from them. His response would not be the one she wanted; it never would be. "Zane and I have been discussing it on and off for a while now. Neither of us is ever home much. We're always traveling somewhere or spending hours on end at work, yet I have an apartment in New York, and he owns a house here in the San Francisco area. As you know, some friends of his are staying at his place until they complete the renovations on their home," he added with a smile, and she responded with one of her own that told him they both knew he wouldn't be living with her if it wasn't the case. "Anyway, we agreed that I would give up my place in New York since I only rent, and I could move my stuff into his house. He's tired of trying to maintain the place when he's gone, and he thinks between the two of us, we can take care of it." He pushed aside the sense of loss he felt whenever he thought about his inevitable move from Kimberly's house.

"I've decided to go to New York this weekend to clear out my apartment. Zane is going to call his friends and let them know they should expect a few boxes to be delivered. The timing is right, my lease is up at the end of the month, and, well, I might as well, while I have the time." And I need to put some distance between us. We both need a break, and it's for the best, he mentally added. Trust me, please.

"Sounds like as good a plan as any."

He looked at her, and he swore she wanted to say something else, but when she didn't, he said, "Yeah, I think it will work out okay. Especially since Zane plans to be home in another four or five weeks, and I promised my producer I would be back to work in another month, two at the most. Gramps will be glad to have Zane around, especially while I'm off to the Middle East again for at least six months."

"Like I said, sounds like as good of a plan as any," she repeated with a shrug. She unfolded her legs and sat up on her knees and the balls of her feet. She packed her camera back into its case and placed it into a large canvas bag.

Jake admitted he was disappointed by her lack of reaction, but knew it was for the best. He had spent the morning beating himself up over his behavior last night, so her indifference should be a welcome relief. But it wasn't, and it scared the hell out of him.

"I think Daisy has had enough of the heat. I better get going" she added without a glance in his direction.

Lost in his thought, it took him several moments before he followed her lead and jumped up to help her fold the blanket.

"Thanks, Jake," she murmured when he offered to carry the cooler and blanket home for her. "Come on, Daisy," she cooed to the large dog. "Tell the ducks you'll see them tomorrow."

"I think they would rather hear her say goodbye, as in forever," Jake joked and handed Daisy's leash to her.

"You're probably right," she laughed easily, and they walked side by side, along the gravel path that led them out of the park.

They walked for several blocks in silence until Jake finally spoke up a few yards away from her house. "You know, Kim, when you told Daisy to tell the ducks that she will see them tomorrow, it reminded me of something I've wanted to ask you about."

"Yes?"

"I have noticed that you never say 'goodbye.' I mean, maybe it's just a coincidence, but you always say 'see you tomorrow,' or 'talk to you later,' even on the phone." He glanced at her, and her expression was amused. "You think I'm crazy for bringing it up, don't you? Blame it on the inquisitive habits of a journalist. We analyze and take note of everything." He turned his head to look at her and found her smiling back at him, her dark eyes sparkling.

"No, I don't think you're crazy." She laughed and pulled on Daisy's leash to prevent her from trampling some flowers. "But you're going to think I am."

"Try me."

"Well, it's sort of a superstition I picked up from my grandma."

"Grandma Lily, I presume?"

"The one and the same," she answered. Her eyes danced with merriment, and he looked away before he became completely lost in them. There couldn't be a repeat of last night's performance. He couldn't let that happen again.

"Anyway, Grandma Lily never said, 'goodbye,' nor did she allow anyone else to say it to her. She insisted that 'goodbye' was too permanent, like forever, whereas, 'see you later,' always promised a tomorrow, you know, like you'd see each other again. It's crazy, but it's always stuck with me. I don't know if I'm superstitious or just acting out of respect for my grandma. Can you tell I adored the eccentric, old woman?" she added with a laugh.

"Yeah, I sure can." He sighed deeply as they climbed the steps of her front porch. He was disturbed by her explanation. He sensed somehow that it was some type of foreshadowing for their relationship. He placed the blanket and cooler on the kitchen table, and then he mumbled a hasty excuse to Kimberly and retreated to his room. For the rest of the evening, he couldn't shake off the uneasiness he had felt after their conversation.

Chapter 7

Jake grabbed the brightly wrapped package from the front seat of the car and then handed the valet the keys to his car. He glanced at the large, stone building façade and recalled the awe that had overcome him on his first visit to the Oaks Country Club almost twenty years ago. Tall, ornately carved pillars proudly supported the massive structure that boasted a long, winding balcony. The wide front stair case looked as if it belonged in front of the White House, instead of a California country club. Acres of plush, green grass surrounded the building, and thousands of colorful flowers lined the sidewalks.

Laughter, mingled with the muffled sound of music, echoed around him as he climbed the steps to the front entrance. Small, intimate groups of three or four people gathered on the balcony, and their voices filled the night air. From the distance, only their silhouettes, and none of their faces, were visible to him. He clutched the package tightly in his hand. Somewhere, amongst the many guests attending various events at the country club, was Kimberly.

After he discovered the Urbane party was in the Almond Room, he walked with purposeful strides through one of the country club's winding hallways. He could not deny why he was back in California so soon, not even to himself. During the entire flight from New York, he had thought of little else but seeing Kimberly this evening, eager to witness the surprise in her exquisite brown eyes when he walked through the banquet room door. He hadn't planned on attending her brother's birthday party and had told her this much earlier in the week. He had plans to be in New York for the weekend, and he couldn't change them. Yet, here he was, at George's party, back from New York less than thirty-six hours from the time he had left San Francisco.

He had convinced himself that the constant torture of wanting something he couldn't have was the reason for his reckless actions. He had become a man possessed by an exotic creature who invaded his being so thoroughly that he had been virtually useless over the past two days.

He had packed his apartment's meager belongings into a half a dozen boxes and a few suitcases and accomplished little else during his trip. For a day and a half, he did little more than mope around his apartment thinking about her; he even missed taking Daisy for walks.

At a local neighborhood bar with friends the night before, he had found himself unable to take an interest in any of the women who made eye contact with him. Each time his friends had commented on a particularly stunning brunette or an attractive blonde, he didn't even bother to glance in her direction. His thoughts were occupied with Kimberly, his mind lost in visions of her scantily dressed body in a bikini top and jean shorts or in a pair of white jeans that molded themselves to her long legs. Before he could stop himself, he had decided to cut his trip to New York short and return to California.

He had tried to tell himself that he needed to get back to San Francisco for the sake of his grandfather, that the old man would be upset because he missed the visits, but Jake couldn't even fool himself into believing it. Granted, his grandfather would probably cuss him out for his two-day absence on his next visit, but the truth was, he had returned because he missed Kimberly.

Even though their relationship was on shaky grounds, and they had barely spoken to each other since their late-night encounter in the kitchen almost a week ago, he needed to see her. He needed to smell the heady scent of her perfume lingering in a room that she had just vacated. He needed to hear her soft laughter when she played with Daisy in the backyard. He swam in dangerous waters and would likely drown any minute, but he didn't care, not right now, not while he still had time before he left on his next assignment. He wouldn't return to the Middle East until Zane came back, at least for another month, over thirty long days away.

She's a temporary fascination that I need to get out of my system. That's all, he reminded himself again. He had spent the return flight working it out in his head. Kimberly would realize it was the same for her, he reasoned. He was a crush from her childhood, and eventually she would figure it out and grow tired of him. They would each go their separate ways, and neither of them would get hurt in the process. No harm, no foul, he rationalized.

He took a deep breath as he spotted the Almond Room off to his right. Linda Urbane stood at the entrance door and was the first to greet him. "Hi Jake." She cheerfully reached over to place a chaste kiss on his cheek.

"Hi. Sorry I'm late." He shifted the gift to his opposite arm and ran his hand down the front of his jeans in an effort to calm his nerves. Maybe he should have given into protocol after all and worn a suit, he debated with a grudge. Most comfortable in a sports coat and jeans, he had decided earlier to hell with social etiquette and had gone with the jeans. Of course, he could have chosen to wear something else besides a pair of black, scuffed cowboy boots, but his attire was the last thing on his mind this evening.

"Don't worry about arriving late, Jake. I was thrilled when I received your text tonight. I hope your grandfather is well?"

Jake nodded absently. "Yes, he's been doing much better the last few days. I finished my business in New York a little early, that's all. Thank you for asking," he answered sincerely. "Quite a turnout this evening." His eyes darted around the large banquet room for the second time and still hadn't spotted Kimberly.

"Yes, it is. I think there's nearly a hundred people tonight and all for George's thirty-fifth birthday. Imagine the party I'll have to throw him when he turns forty. We'll probably have to rent the entire club out for a week." She laughed and smiled back at him. "Kimberly took some wonderful shots of George and his shock when he walked into the party tonight," she added.

"I'm sure," he responded, with what he hoped was a note of indifference. He searched the room again. "Kimberly's a great photographer. I'm not surprised that they turned out well."

Linda tilted her head, and her eyes sparkled when she looked at him. "George is over by the bar, if that's who you're looking for?

Jake glanced back at her. If she knew he had been searching for Kimberly, she had the grace to keep it to herself.

"Of course, it's the birthday boy... who else would it be?" He looked across the room. "I think I will wish him a happy birthday now," he answered before he excused himself and walked away.

"Jake. Glad you could make it." George reached behind him and a grabbed a drink off the bar. "Beer okay? Or should I order you something else?"

"Beer's fine. I heard you were rather surprised." Jake laughed at the look of embarrassment on his friend's face.

"Hell, yes. Although, I'm still trying to figure out why Linda decided on a surprise party for my thirty-fifth. I've narrowed it down to either she thinks I won't make it to my fortieth, or she's expecting me to throw her a surprise party for her birthday next year."

"Let's hope it's because she wants a surprise party." Jake reached out and patted George on the back. He took a drink of beer as he glanced over George's shoulder to a group of people standing behind him.

"Linda tells me you have been staying with Kimberly since you've been in town? Funny, neither of you mentioned it until recently." George turned around and grabbed a beer for himself off of the bar.

Am I that easy to read? Jake thought crossly, even as he caught himself taking another quick sweep of the room in search of Kimberly. He needed to seriously question how it was that he made a living as an investigative reporter, if he was as open of a book as the Urbanes made him feel like tonight.

"Ah, yeah, I am. Probably for another month. It's close to my grandfather's rehab center, and I had been having a difficult time finding an apartment that I liked." He swiftly drained his glass and placed it on the bar. The bartender caught his eye, and Jake declined the offer with a shake of his head.

"That's what Carly's been telling me. So, what house repairs has Kimberly conned you into doing?" George chuckled in response to Jake's startled expression.

"Come on, Jake, tell me. Have you replaced the deck off of the kitchen? Or how about repairing the crack in her dining room ceiling? I know there has to be something that she hasn't swindled Dad or me into doing yet, especially since I haven't heard from her in over a month. I should have known something was up, just by that alone."

Jake mumbled the list of repairs he willingly volunteered to do around the house and admitted that half of the time, he had had to argue with the little con artist to convince her to let him do them. He accepted that he had been duped and joined George in a good laugh at his own expense. Kimberly, he learned, was excellent at twisting the men in her life around her little finger. When George finally steered the subject away from his sister to something else a few minutes later, Jake was grateful. George could have delivered the "I'm her big brother/she's my little sister, and I'll kill you if you hurt her" speech to him, and it would have been deserved, especially after their encounter in the kitchen last week.

"That gift wouldn't be for me, would it?" George asked with a wide grin and a nod to the package Jake had placed on top of the bar.

"As a matter of fact, it is." Jake nodded and handed him the gift.

"Jake, this is great." He set the discarded wrapping paper on the bar. "I don't know what to say. How did you get your hands on this?" He asked with a tinge of awe in his voice, his eyes glued to the autographed baseball.

"A couple of New York Yankees live in my apartment building. I explained your lasting devotion to their team, and they happily obliged me with some signatures."

"I can't wait to show this to Bob Carlson. He's always bragging to everyone about his baseball collection. Excuse me Jake, while I run over to Bob and do a little boasting. Thanks again!"

Jake smiled at George's eager departure, pleased that he appreciated the gift as much as he did. Jake laughed to himself. His doubts about giving a grown man an autographed baseball were all for nothing. He decided to walk the room when he spotted her.

His eyes nearly doubled in size when he saw her walk across the room, deep in conversation with an older woman whom he didn't recognize. He smoothed a trembling hand across his jaw line. Kim took away his breath. Her hair was pulled into a loose chignon at the back of her head. Several long, curly strands of hair escaped the upsweep and cascaded down her back.

He had thought nothing could be more enticing than seeing her poured into a pair of tight jeans and a snug fitting shirt. He now knew that he had been wrong. Dead wrong. He reached for his beer before he realized he had put the empty glass down and hadn't ordered another one.

Two thin straps held up a black dress that clung to her. The dress' tight bodice accentuated her full, ripe breasts, before it narrowed to emphasize her slim waist. The silky material ended at the middle of her thighs to reveal much of her long slender legs. Her only jewelry was a pair of earrings, dozens of tiny freshwater pearls that sparkled against her golden skin and black hair.

Jake swallowed uneasily as he followed her progress. His pulse raced as he watched the older woman leave Kimberly's side to be replaced by a man he didn't recognize. He clenched his fists at his sides as he witnessed the stranger remove the champagne glass from her hand and escort her onto the dance floor. Disgusted by the tender smile she provided her dance partner as he whirled her around the room, Jake decided to take a walk out onto the terrace to grab some fresh air.

"You've been here less than half of an hour, and already you're hiding out on the balcony?" a familiar voice asked him.

"I've never been one for crowds." Jake turned his head to the side to look at Carly. Dressed in black also, it was obvious why she had been a successful model for so long, before she gave it all up for motherhood. Her wholesome, Christie Brinkley looks contrasted perfectly with her floor-length gown. Stunningly beautiful, she was simply Carly in his eyes, the little sister he never had.

"I saw the autographed baseball you gave George. He's running around the party like a little kid showing it off to everyone."

"Good, I'm glad he liked it." He turned to lean on the balcony railing and inhaled a deep breath of air.

"Jake, I saw you watching Kimberly on the dance floor."

He kept his gaze locked on her. Her blue eyes stared directly back at him, her brows furrowed with concern. "And?"

"And, she snapped at me when I asked her about you tonight. Jake, I... I don't want her to get hurt," she added with a hint of apprehension in her voice. She stared at the small tick in his cheek, and he lifted his hand to the spot to try and stop it.

"I know it's a little late to be thinking about that, particularly after I'm the one who thought up the whole scheme of renting a room from her," she rushed on.

His eyebrows arched high on his forehead. A little late? he wanted to sarcastically retort, but held his tongue.

"I realize now that maybe it wasn't such a good idea. I mean you two aren't serious, are you?" She chewed nervously on her lower lip, and he turned his back on her.

The moonlight glistened on the perfectly manicured lawn in front of them, and the beauty was lost on him. He laughed harshly and shook his head in a slow, purposeful response. "Nope." Carly leaned against the railing only a few inches away from him, and his gaze remained unwavering.

"Carly," he said, his voice distant and cool, "I'm an international journalist, traveling all over the world for months at a time. I don't have time for serious relationships." Especially not with a raven-haired beauty that causes my heart to stop and makes it difficult to breathe without concentrating. "Besides," he replied in hardly more than a whisper and turned his head to look at her, "You know better than anyone that I'll never remarry. I almost ruined one woman's life and nearly killed myself with guilt in the process. I won't let history repeat itself, and please don't pretend that you don't know what I'm talking about. I know you eavesdropped on our conversation, the night George and I got drunk at Erica and Cody's wedding, and I poured my guts out to him about my divorce."

Carly stared into her water glass. She absently swirled the glass around in her hand.

"Carly, look at me. Look at me, and tell me straight to my face that your sister could live her life without children. Do it, Carly."

Carly lifted her head. Tears pooled in the corner of her eyes. "I, ah, you know I can't, Jake." Her eyes darted to the space around his head until they finally landed on his face again. "But I'm not the one you should be asking. If you really care about Kimberly, you should be having this discussion with her, not me." She reached out and placed her hand on his upper arm. "She might surprise you."

Jake's laughter was filled with bitterness. He realized now that coming here this evening was a mistake. Carly was right in her concerns for her sister. He would hurt her in the end, once he walked away from her for good. "Look, Carly. I do care about your sister, and she's a wonderful person. But that's it. I like my life the way it is, and Kimberly is not part of it, not beyond that of a friend and a landlord," he bit out harder than he intended. Feeling guilty for his harsh response, he leaned over to ruffle the top of her hair, as he had often done when she was a child, but patted her on the shoulder instead because she would likely swat his hand away from her perfectly coiffed hair. "Come on, Carly. Let's go back inside and join the party."

Carly searched his eyes for several moments and finally nodded before she followed him back into the large banquet room.

Jake spent the next thirty minutes mingling with party guests. His mood temporarily lifted after his conversation with Carly. He needed to hear that a relationship with Kimberly was impossible, even if the words had to come from his own mouth.

Whether he was purposely avoiding Kimberly, or she was avoiding him, he still hadn't figured out nearly an hour later. Finally, unable to watch her attention monopolized for another minute by Conner, the identity of her constant companion he learned from another guest, he decided it was time for them to acknowledge each other. After all, they lived together, something Conner surely didn't know, Jake thought with a smile to himself. His grin was still in place when he approached the pair of them minutes later.

"Hello, Kimberly." His gaze traveled over her creamy skin and then to the black dress that molded itself to her lean curves. He found it hard to believe that she could be even more beautiful up close than she was from across the room. She was, and he was having a hard time trying to ignore the fact.

"Jake." Her dark eyes lit up in surprise. "I, ah, thought you were in New York until Monday?"

Jake swore swiftly under his breath. Incredible. She hadn't even known that he was at the party until now, and he had been in attendance for over an hour. He could tell by the slur in her voice that she had had far too much to drink, and he blamed it on the Nordic giant who stood at her side and had plied her with drinks all night. Conner, even his name irritated Jake. He hated Conner on sight.

He stared back at her without blinking an eye. "I came back early. I knew how much you wanted me to come with you tonight, and I was determined not to disappoint you."

He returned her smile with one of his own, although his lacked the drunken twist at its corners that hers had, while irritation emanated from every one of his pores. The confused look occupying her face confirmed that she had had more to drink than he first guessed. He inwardly groaned when she covered her mouth with her hand to stifle a hiccup.

"I apologize." Jake smiled mockingly at Conner. "I haven't introduced myself. I'm Jake Taylor. I live with Kimberly." He held his hand out to the other man, while he ignored Kimberly's swift intake of breath followed by another hiccup.

"Conner Douglas." The tall, well-dressed investment banker extended his hand out to Jake, while he inched away from Kimberly.

"Pleasure to meet you. I hope you don't mind if I excuse myself and get another drink?" Conner turned to walk away, but not before he gave Kimberly a distinctive snort of disgust. Jake hid his laughter behind a fake cough.

"How dare you, Jake!" Kimberly hissed under her breath. "I can't believe you said that to him. No, I can't believe the *way* you said that to him. I'm sure Conner thinks that we're, you know, living together, living together." She exhaled deeply in an attempt to blow at a large curly lock of hair that had escaped her chignon and now fell softly against her cheek. Jake reached up and pushed the strand of hair to behind her ear.

"You're not making any sense, Kimberly." He cocked his head and intentionally gave her a blank stare. "We are living together."

"Ugh," she growled in frustration. "You know perfectly well what I mean, and you did that on purpose. Conner has been a gentleman all evening, and you've gone and scared him away." She reached for a champagne glass from a passing waiter, and he brushed her hand away.

"You've had too much to drink already, and Conner is not a gentleman." His eyes narrowed over his brows, and he moved closer to her side. His voice was hard and exact when he spoke again. "From what little I've learned about the guy this evening, he goes through women like they are different courses of a meal. Tonight, he chose you as his main entrée."

"You don't know what you're talking about, Jake Taylor! Conner is a business associate of George's and also a friend of his," she tartly informed him with a tilt of her chin.

"Who do you think I got my information from?" He sneered at her with a sardonic grin. "You can be so naïve."

"What did you say?" she practically screeched and placed a hand on each of her slender hips. Her black eyes blazed back at him.

"You obviously heard me, Kimberly. Don't give me that look. I said you can be naïve, and it's the truth. You're dressed in a slinky black slip that exposes more than it covers, and you've drunk a gallon of champagne tonight. What do you think Conner had in mind this evening, a chaste kiss at your doorstep after driving you home? Give me a break."

"How do you know that I didn't want to spend the night with Conner? Maybe I wanted more than just a chaste kiss at my doorstep?"

Jakes eyes narrowed. "Of that, I have no doubt. You have clung to him for the past hour like you couldn't wait for him to take you home. Be grateful that I saved you from embarrassing your family any further by interfering when I did."

"I have not embarrassed my family this evening," she snapped. "You don't know what you're talking about—"

"Really?" he interrupted. "Why don't you take a look around you. More than a few people are staring at us right now." He nodded to several groups of people in various places around the room.

"If anyone is causing a scene, it's you, and I refuse to let anyone think I'm to blame for your rude behavior."

Jake's eyes narrowed into mere slits as he enunciated each word in a deadly calm voice, "You're damn right you're not, because I'm not giving you the chance. We're leaving. I'm telling Carly that I'm taking you home. She'll understand that you have had far too much to drink and will be grateful to me. Don't even try to argue with me." Jake clenched his hands into tight fists at his sides.

Kimberly opened her mouth to protest and then snapped it shut. "Fine," she agreed in an indignant huff. He stared at her for several moments, daring her to say anything else, before he turned and walked away.

"Let's go," he said a few minutes later after helping her find her purse from underneath a table.

"Jake," she began once they were driving down the highway.

"Forget it, Kimberly. I refuse to argue with you while I'm driving."

Clearly frustrated with him, Kimberly stared out the car window for the remainder of the trip home.

Once inside the house, they each went their separate ways. Kimberly intentionally pounded up the stairs in her high heels, while Jake went into the living room.

Jake threw his blazer down over the arm of the couch and unbuttoned the top button of his shirt with a long sigh. He put some music on, and the mellow jazz filtered throughout the room, its soft melody instantly relaxing him. He sat down on the couch and removed his boots, carelessly tossing them aside without a thought. He was angry, angry with himself for allowing Kimberly to affect him the way she did, angry that he had expected, hell, he didn't know what he had expected tonight, but it hadn't been to find her with another man at the party.

Edgy and sorely in need of a drink, Jake decided to prepare himself a healthy glass of scotch. Hopefully, with any luck, he would pass out on the couch, blocking all thoughts of Kimberly from his mind. He heard a movement by the bar just as he leaned his head against the back of the couch and closed his eyes. He turned swiftly in the direction of the noise and saw Kimberly.

"Why aren't you asleep?" he asked irritably. She was still in the little black number she had worn to the party, but had removed her heels. Additional strands of her hair had escaped from her chignon to lay softly against the base of her neck. He took a deep breath of air as he allowed his eyes to travel over her legs, their slenderness accentuated by the dress swishing against her skin.

"I couldn't sleep. I thought I would have a glass of wine before I went to bed." She held up her hand to stop him. "Before you say anything, don't bother. I'm thirty-one years old. I'm allowed to drink if I want, to get rip-roaring drunk if I choose to." She glared back at him and then reached for a bottle of wine off of the rack in the bar.

"The hell you are." He shot upright and stood up. "If you think I'm going to sit and watch you drink a bottle of wine and then stay up babysitting you for the rest of the night, you can forget it." He breached the distance between them with two powerful strides. He reached across her, his hand brushing against the bare skin of her arm as he wrenched the unopened bottle of wine from her hands.

She trembled at his touch, and he felt a similar shiver travel up his own skin from their brief contact. She was practically sober now. Her previous slur was absent from the lecture she had just given him, which rattled him even more than if she were drunk. Sober, there was no excuse for her actions or her reaction to him.

She turned to look at him. "Don't try to bully me, Jake Taylor." She lunged for the bottle of wine. "Just give me the damn bottle," she lashed out.

Jake watched the fire glowing from her dark eyes as she struggled against him for the bottle of wine. The air around him grew warm as he glanced at her heaving breasts, much of them exposed in her low-cut dress. The moonlight streamed through the window and shone on her creamy shoulders, begging him, he swore, to taste them with his lips. He released his hold on the bottle of wine, and his gaze traveled upward to look deeply into her eyes.

Jake watched her reaction, the slow realization that he had stopped fighting her finally dawning on her. Her dark eyes searched his for answers. "Jake?" she asked hesitantly.

"Kim," he whispered before bending his head toward her. He took the wine bottle from her hands and placed it down on the bar as his mouth brushed against hers. His lips moved softly against hers, and he gently eased them open with a slow devouring of her mouth. His hands held onto the sides of her waist, crushing her to him as he deepened their kiss with exhilarating momentum.

His hands caressed their way up her back until they reached her hair. With one swift motion, he removed the clip from her hair and the dark mane cascaded down her back. She pushed her pelvis into his pounding arousal, and he growled with satisfaction.

Kimberly moaned with pleasure when he released her lips to allow his mouth to explore the pulsing hollow at the base of her throat. Her body trembled under his fingers when he pushed the tiny straps of her dress from her shoulders. He eased the zipper of her dress down her back, and she groaned evocatively into his ear. The dressed slipped away from her skin, landing in a soft puddle at her ankles.

Jake groaned with pleasure upon the discovery that she was braless, his breath a series of short, raspy gasps. Her rosy nipples were hard and pointed when he brought his hands between their bodies to cup each of her full, milky-white breasts.

She trembled under his touch, and he realized that he went too fast, much too fast with her. This is Kimberly, he reminded himself, when she dragged her nails over the front of his chest, and an unexpected rush of pleasure flowed through his veins. She wasn't a one-night stand on which to take out his pent-up frustrations. She was a beautiful, elegant woman, a woman he laid awake thinking about at night, envisioning himself taking her into his arms as he did right now.

Taking a deep, tortured breath, he forced himself to slow down, despite the wild pounding of his heart. His tongue traveled in slow, rhythmic circles down her neck and over her breasts until he took a pink tip into his mouth. She squirmed beneath his touch, and he felt her knees go weak in response.

Swiftly he released his hold on her and reached for a blanket from the back of a chair, spreading it on the floor next to them. Slowly, gently, he lowered her to the floor with him. He lay down next to her, propped up on his elbow. Kimberly lay on her back wearing only a pair of black lace panties, her eyes glazed with passion as she looked up at him.

He ran his finger along the flat contours of her stomach, reveling in the tiny shivers her body released each time he touched a sensitive area on her skin. He leaned over her and placed soft kisses on her face, along the fine bones defining her cheeks and brow. His hand continued to caress the hollow of her abdomen as he nuzzled her earlobe.

He felt her fingertips tremble against the skin on his neck until they wound themselves together at the back of his head and, released his hair from its confining leather band. His hair dangled wildly to brush his shoulders, and she ran her fingers through the loose strands.

Pleased by her initiative, Jake raised his gaze to stare directly into her eyes. He searched her face for any sign of rejection, anything to indicate that he should put a halt to their lovemaking.

He found none.

With one swift, fluid motion, he sat up and began to unbutton his shirt. Kimberly watched his progress with hungry eyes, and he was pleased. She drew her tongue over her swollen lips when his shirt slipped from his chest and onto the floor. He grinned down at her. "I... you're, you're beautiful, Jake."

"I hardly compare to you, Kim." His voice was heavy- laden with the passion that consumed him. He could never tire of looking at her.

Kimberly's eyes glowed, while she ran a long, painted fingernail along the matte chest hair, and he shut his eyes. She sat up, and he realized she was eager to take a more aggressive role in their lovemaking.

She pushed his hands away from the waistband of his pants and though her hands were obviously trembling, she unbuttoned his jeans and eased the zipper down over his throbbing arousal. He opened his eyes and stared back at her. She raised an eyebrow, and her look dared him to stop her. He didn't, and to his pleasure, she bent her head and pressed a smattering of feathery kisses upon his chest.

Jake moaned as she continued to lower his jeans over his hips, and his hardened manhood pounded in desire. He was near collapse when he felt her soft fingertips trace the outline of him through his boxer briefs. Afraid that their lovemaking would end in mere seconds, he could no longer able to allow her to be the aggressor and gently coaxed her to lie on her back. He bent his head to her stomach and his tongue darted out to explore the hollow of her abdomen and hipbones. He slid her lace panties from her body and then removed the remainder of his own clothing.

"Jake, we're not using any, any protection," she whispered between gasping breaths.

"It's okay, trust me." He took a swollen nipple between his teeth. He visibly panted, and knew he was not alone in his desire when he slid his hand between her legs.

All thoughts of birth control must have disappeared from her thoughts, he realized, because she arched into his hand. "Jake," she screamed when his fingers continued to move within the soft folds of her skin. She was more than ready for him to be inside her. "You're so warm, so tight," he whispered huskily into her mouth. He covered her mouth with his own as he entered her and gradually eased himself into her silky depths. He was grateful for her moan of pleasure, eager to bring her to the next height of their lovemaking.

He played a sexual dance with her. He slowly retreated, then quickly plunged back into her over and over again. Kimberly wrapped her long legs higher and arched her hips into him. Sweat glistened her brow, and he wiped it away with his fingertips. "Jake," she cried out as he plunged into her the last time, and her body climaxed with wild abandon. Somewhere in the deep recesses of his mind, he heard her call out his name.

Jake, shaken from the aftermath of their lovemaking, was unable to believe he could feel the way he did. Never had it been so complete, felt so right before. Kimberly had taken him to places he never dreamed possible. He lowered himself next to her and swept her tightly into his embrace. He held her against his sweat-glistening body and placed tender kisses in her tangled hair.

Kimberly sighed deeply. He heard her murmur his name before she fell asleep within the confines of his arms. The soft sound of her breathing hit a deep cord within him. He watched the moonlight shine through the window with unblinking eyes and knew with a disturbing realization that sleep would elude him for a long time.

Chapter 8

Jake lay awake in bed, temporarily mesmerized by the stark contrast of Kimberly's black hair against the white pillowcases. They had moved to her bed during the night after both agreeing that the living room floor was comfortable for only so long. He watched the fall and rise of her breasts, partially covered by the sheet, while she slept curled up at his side. He felt a contentment he had never experienced before in his life. It scared the hell out of him because he actually felt a glimmer of hope for a future that he once thought was an impossibility. Carly's advice from the previous night echoed through his brain as he smoothed a soft curl away from Kimberly's face. *She may surprise you,* he heard over and over again.

Kimberly lay nestled against him, and he raked his fingers through his hair with his hand, pushing the long strands behind his ear. For the past hour, his mind had been a mental war zone of conflicting emotions. Her sister had been right, he conceded. Kimberly had surprised him. She surprised him by the way she had loved him during the night, touching a place in him no other woman ever had. He need only to run his hand along her smooth curves to convince himself that it could work between them, that somehow, some way a union between them was possible. Then, just as quickly, a dark cloud would overshadow his thoughts with haunting excerpts from his past that came back in frightening clarity.

He visibly winced. His ex's hateful accusations taunted him. Twice during the past hour, he had pressed Kimberly closer into his embrace to reassure himself that the ugly memories from his marriage were only that, memories. Kimberly was different; she was nothing like his ex, and he placed a gentle kiss on the top of her head to remind himself of that. He breathed deeply, while his conscience mocked that he had once thought Brenda was different as well.

Jake pulled the white linen sheet over Kimberly's back when he felt her stir. What am I going to do? he asked himself when she began to show signs of waking. He couldn't leave her feeling as if last night had meant nothing more than a causal tumble in the sack, but what he could he say? He couldn't blurt out the truth and tell her that he was terrified of a relationship with her, terrified of the hurt and degradation he would inevitably feel when she rejected him because he could never truly be the husband she wanted, the husband to give her the children she rightly deserved. Kimberly was a passionate, loving person, as she had proved to him over and over again during the night. She would have enough love for a dozen children and still burst at the seams with more.

"*She may surprise you,*" Carly's voice taunted his subconscious. Kimberly stretched a long, willowy leg against the side of his calf, and he decided to tell her. Talk to her while you have the chance, his heart willed, as his conscience begged him not to take the risk. A cold shiver rippled along his skin when Kimberly brought her hand to settle on the middle of his chest.

Jake took a large gulp of air. He would tell her now, just as soon as he could think straight enough to concentrate, he determined with a groan. His body responded to the sensations caused by her wandering hand, and coherent thought was no longer an option.

"Mmm, cold Jake?" Kimberly purred and snuggled closer into his warmth. She rubbed her toes against the hard length of his naked leg and purred seductively into his ear. He thought his passion was sated, convinced that his ardor would be content with the numerous times they had made love during the night. He was wrong, growing increasingly aroused by the idea of making love with her again. She moaned against his chest, and he ached to be inside her again, to bring her to a dimension of arousal he hoped she had only dreamed of before last night.

She raised her leg, the apex of her thighs wet against his skin, and she nudged herself closer to him, her bare stomach and breasts pressed softly against the hard planes of his chest and ribcage. Her hair lay blanketed across her shoulders and back. One hand lay tucked underneath her cheek, while her other hand explored his chest.

"Not anymore," Jake replied. Kimberly's fingertips traveled a dangerous path over his body, one that caused his heart to pound rapidly in his chest. He leaned over and kissed her forehead while her hand continued to wander downward. Unable to take much more of her fingernails drawing circles along his abdomen, sure he knew their final destination, Jake reached over and grasped her slender hip. With one strong hand, he drew her over him to lay her flush with his own body.

"Good morning." He captured her lips in a sensuous kiss.

Kimberly slowly opened her eyes, and her pupils dilated to adjust to the bright sunlight streaming through the window. Her creamy thighs straddled his torso, and the tips of her breasts brushed wickedly against his chest. She hungrily returned his kiss while she ran fingers through his hair.

Jake smoothed his hands along her smooth back and caressed the velvety skin along her spine. He growled with an unsatiated need as Kimberly's lips released his own to place soft, wet kisses along his razor-stubbled jawbone.

"Good morning, yourself," she finally answered and moved her tongue sensually along the curves of his earlobe. She adjusted her body lower and pressed the wet, moist area at the joining of her thighs against his hard, throbbing arousal. Back and forth, she caressed his pounding manhood, and a hot stream of excitement flowed through his veins.

"Kim." His hands tightened around her taut buttock muscles, the last of his control slipping away. In one swift motion, he lifted her hips above him, bringing her down on his hard, throbbing erection. Sweat dripped off of his forehead as he lifted his hips, grinding himself deep inside of her.

Kimberly gasped, and sat up straight to allow her body to sit perpendicular to his torso, taking him fully inside of her. She rocked up and down, and as he cupped each of her breasts in his hands, his thumbs caressed her nipples into hard nubs. She screamed as he plunged deeper, and he felt his manhood press against her womb. "Jake," she cried wildly, as she continued to rock her hips.

Jake shook as he spilled his seed into her, and Kimberly's own climax followed closely behind. Her body convulsed around him, until she lay limply draped over him. He drew her close against his chest and wrapped his arms around her. He kissed her forehead, damp with perspiration.

"That was one hell of a good morning kiss."

"Mmm," she murmured contentedly in his arms. She wiggled closer into his warmth, the top of her head nestled against the column of his throat, and he took the opportunity to press a lingering kiss to the top of her head. Her deep sigh had been barely audible over the sound of his beating chest pounding in his ears.

"Just think." He paused and trailed his fingertip along her cheek. "In another half an hour, it will be time for a good afternoon kiss." He chuckled softly before running his fingers through her long, curly hair spread across both of their naked bodies.

"Mmm." Almost instantly, every muscle in her body tensed. "What did you say?" She lifted her head to look at him.

"An afternoon kiss, Kim. It's eleven-thirty. We slept the morning away." He laughed at the sudden widening of her dark, sultry eyes.

"Slept the morning away!" She pulled her long limbs from around him and scrambled to get off the bed. "George's birthday party. I forgot that I promised Linda I would take pictures. Yikes. I'm supposed to be there by one o'clock," she rambled and ran her fingers through her tangled hair.

"Slow down, Kim. You're not making any sense. George's party was last night. What are you talking about?" he asked.

"Today's the kids' party, you know, balloons, cake. That sort of stuff. The family type of thing. I promised Linda I would take pictures. She particularly wants me to try to get a family shot of George and her and the kids. Darn, I'm going to be late," she muttered.

"Oh."

"You'll come with me, won't you?" She paused at the bedroom door. "I mean, you're welcome to come. I didn't mention it before because I thought you would still be in New York."

Jake, now propped up against several pillows, bent his head back to stare up at the ceiling. He had finally made the decision to risk the possibility of a future for them together, and their discussion was being postponed by a kids' party. The irony was not lost on him. Postponed only until tonight, he promised himself.

He lifted his head up and glanced over at her. He traced the long, winding curves of her naked body with his eyes and felt himself grow hard again.

"What the hell. Since I missed out on a piece of birthday cake last night, I guess I owe it to myself today." He grinned broadly at her.

"Great." A grin teased the corner of her lips. "Jake." She tilted her head at him and tossed back her hair behind her shoulder. "If you think it will get us out of here sooner, you're welcome to join me in the shower."

Jake smirked cockily. He needn't waste any time to consider the best offer he had had in a long time. He nearly stumbled over his own feet, as he raced into the bathroom after her.

****

"Sweetheart, why don't you come inside with Auntie Kimberly, and I'll get you a bandage. Maybe mommy has some of those bandages with Mickey Mouse on them. How's that? Will that make you feel better?" Kimberly cooed to her three-year-old niece, Maggie, who now sported a scraped knee from trying to keep up with her older brother in a game of tag. Nodding her head, with two curly ponytails positioned high above each ear, the small child wrapped her arms around her aunt's neck. Kimberly smiled over her niece's head at Jake.

Jake watched as Kim placed a gentle kiss on Maggie's forehead before scooping the child into her arms and heading in the direction of the house.

Jake stood at the gas grill with a spatula dangling from his hand. He was alone now, having volunteered to watch over the barbecue, while George put more beer in the cooler. Jake turned over each of the hamburgers and then closed the grill cover just in time to watch Kimberly walk into the house with her niece cuddled in her arms. He felt his stomach muscles tighten at the sight of their two curly, black heads bent close together, appearing very much like mother and daughter.

He raised his hand and raked several strands of his hair away from his forehead. He should have pulled his hair back in this heat. He was irritated and disgusted to admit that he hadn't because Kimberly told him she liked it down and loose. Maybe he would just cut it all off and get a crewcut for all he cared at the moment. It had taken an afternoon of watching Kimberly with George's children to realize that he had deluded himself about any possibility of a relationship with her. It would never work, just as it hadn't worked with his ex-wife.

George's kids clung to their Aunt Kimberly, particularly the little girl, Maggie, as if she were their own fairy Godmother. Kimberly's own daughter would look just like her; long black curls would frame a pair of dark, almond-shaped eyes. Her sons would probably have dark hair also, definitely a dominant gene in the Urbane family, having bypassed only Carly. Daughters and sons. Kimberly's daughters and sons. Children she should have, children he couldn't give her.

The strong smell of burning meat permeated the air and forced him to return his attention to the burgers he was supposed to be standing guard over. He was glad for the distraction; it helped push aside a wave of hopelessness that washed over him. At least he had come to a decision over the last half an hour. He wasn't going to have the discussion he had planned with Kimberly tonight. He had been living in a fantasyland for the past twenty-four hours, and it was time to come back to reality. Any chance they might have together was gone, gone with the soft tenderness she displayed when she ran a soothing hand over her niece's cheek or pressed a tender kiss to her forehead.

Jake turned the meat over with a deep sigh. Someday he would be grateful that he had spared his already damaged heart from further injury, even though at the moment, his heart hurt as if it were already beyond repair. He glanced at the glass door that Kimberly and her niece had disappeared through, and he shook his head as a deep sadness engulfed him.

*****

"All better, Maggie? Good girl. Now go out there, and show those boys that you're just as tough as they are." Kimberly quickly placed a kiss on Maggie's cheek before the three-year-old raced out the kitchen sliding glass door.

"She's such a cutie, isn't she?" Carly commented from behind her.

"Yes, she is." She stared out the patio door into the backyard and drew a mental picture of her own children. Perhaps two little girls, maybe three, and a couple of boys. The girls would have black hair like her own, while the boys would have Jake's golden-brown hair. She pictured her sons with hair long enough to brush their shoulders, pushed back from their faces by tiny aviator sunglasses, and laughter bubbled inside of her.

"Kimberly, you made the last pitcher of lemonade, didn't you? I need to make another batch. Can you help me find the mix?" Carly held an empty pitcher in her hand and waited for her sister's response.

"Ah, oh, sure." Kimberly shook herself. She was surprised to find Carly in the room with her, and she knew it was because she had been lost in her daydreaming. A shiver crept through her as she fought to clear the previous images from her mind. Wonderful images, she silently prayed, that foreshadowed her and

Jake's future together. Never had she dared to allow her dreams for the two of them to occupy such a real presence in her mind. The last eighteen hours, most of them spent in Jake's arms, had changed all of that, and she permitted herself the fantasy.

She was not so naïve as to believe that Jake's feelings ran as deep as her own. How could they? She had nearly twenty years of love for him locked away inside of her, some of which she had finally been able to show him when he had taken her into his arms last night, more seeping out of her during the night and then again in the morning. Neither of them had spoken of their feelings to the other, and she suddenly worried over the reason. An uneasiness teased her, despite the recent intimacy they had shared and the contentment she had felt only a few moments ago. An unwanted insecurity developed deep in the pit of her stomach. She needed to find Jake to see the raw passion burn in his eyes for her as it had only hours ago.

Kimberly turned away from the patio door, and with a glance at the interior of the kitchen, she realized she couldn't remember what she was supposed to be looking for.

"I think Linda keeps more lemonade in the pantry," Carly said.

"What? Oh, right." Kimberly nodded and walked over to the pantry. She retrieved the can of powered lemonade and placed it on the countertop before she walked toward the sliding glass door.

"Kimberly?"

"Yeah?"

"I take it you got home all right last night? Jake, he didn't... well... he didn't appear to be happy when you two left. I'm sure he gave you an earful in the car?" Kimberly was quick to shake herself out of her deep thoughts when she turned around to face her sister and found her eyes were narrowed in concern with her finely groomed brows slanted downward.

She and Jake's relationship had reached a turning point last night, and her sister could sense it. Carly had some strange kind of intuitive radar, always had since they were kids. More than a few times throughout the afternoon, Kimberly had caught Carly staring at her, when either she or Jake were stealing glances of one another. And she was the first to admit that she had been unable to hold a sensible conversation with anyone all afternoon. She was far too distracted with thoughts of Jake to focus.

She had intentionally avoided the adults, particularly Carly, by surrounding herself with the children all day. She had avoided each of their questioning glances, especially her sister's, because she was pretty sure that Carly was onto them. Damn, Carly had figured out that the two of them had done a lot more than sleeping last night, and now Kim would receive a lecture from her because of it.

"No, not really. We didn't talk much on the way home," Kimberly answered and quickly turned to leave the room.

"Wait," Carly chirped in a high pitch tone. Carly wrung her hands together, and Kimberly decided to give into her plea. Carly would hunt her down later anyway. She might as well get the torture over with now. "Kimberly, please, I need to talk to you."

Kimberly turned back around to look at her sister. "What is it, Carly?" She was eager to find Jake so she could put her uneasiness aside. Playing twenty questions with Carly was definitely not on her agenda.

"I... Kimberly...I, ah, I'm pretty sure there's something going on between Jake and you," she rushed on. "And well, I don't want you to get hurt, Kimberly. I know how you feel about him, how you felt about him since we were kids. Please be careful, I guess is what I'm trying to say."

"Carly, what exactly are you getting at?" She did not need this right now from her sister, particularly since she was worried about the same thing. She crossed her arms in front of her.

"Kimberly," Carly stated in a soft voice. "I spoke to Jake last night. He was alone out on the terrace. I think you were dancing with George's friend at the time. Anyway, I sort of brought up my reservations about a relationship between the two of you and—"

"You what?" Kimberly blurted, her face flushed with embarrassment. Carly's prying into her life had definitely gone too far this time.

Carly held out her hands in front of her. "Please, let me explain. I feel responsible for getting the two of you together, and well, I know you were upset last night. And, uh, Jake watched you flutter around the dance floor like he wanted to drag you out of there the first chance he got. I had to do something. I thought, maybe he could talk to someone. I don't know."

Carly wrung her hands together again, and she pulled her lower lip between her teeth. She was nervous, but Kimberly didn't care. Her sister had no right to speak to Jake about the two of them. "Carly, how dare you—"

"Kimberly, Jake is returning to the Middle East for at least six months," Carly interrupted. "Do you know what it's like to be separated for that amount of time? Well, believe me. I do. Damien is gone more than he is at home. Sometimes I wish he would give up the band and find a career that keeps him at home. It's really hard, Kimberly. I actually dream about having a real marriage and a husband who's there for me. Then I realize that playing in a band as a bass player was Damien's dream long before I met him, and I can't ask him to give it up. I love him too much to ask him to do anything else."

After a long pause, Carly sighed in a defeated tone. "Forget it. I have no right to be giving you advice, not when my own life is so screwed up. I just want you to be happy." Carly shrugged before she turned around and placed the glass pitcher in the sink. She turned the faucet to cold and began to fill the pitcher with water.

Kimberly's anger drained from her. Carly meant no harm, despite the fear her words added to Kim's own piling list of insecurities. "Hey, Carly," she whispered from behind her sister. "I know a relationship with Jake won't be perfect, but you know what?"

"What?"

"I think he's almost perfect, and I love him. And well, that's good enough for me." Kimberly waited until her younger sister returned her smile before she left the room.

Kimberly closed the patio door behind her, while Carly's words weighed heavily on her mind. She knew Jake was returning to the Middle East. He had told her so himself, but somehow it seemed more real hearing it from someone else. She breathed deeply when she spotted Jake standing by the barbecue. He was everything to her, all she had ever dreamed of and more. Carly was right. She wouldn't want to be separated from Jake for any length of time and certainly not for six months. She didn't think she could survive that length of time without him. He was in her blood now, a part of her as vital as any other part.

She brushed a thick strand of hair from off of her shoulder as an idea formulated in her mind. There was only one thing she could do, she decided determinedly. She was going to have to use every feminine wiles she possessed to get him to stay home. Even if that meant spending endless hours with him in bed, then she would just have to sacrifice herself. She was grinning from ear to ear by the time her niece intercepted her, begging her to play on the swing set with her. She spied Jake in a conversation with her sister-in-law and smiled softly at him. He winked at her and then returned his attention to Linda. She followed on her niece's heels in a far better mood than she had been in only minutes ago. Everything was going to be fine, it really was, she decided with a fluttering in her heart.

****

"Boy, am I beat." Kimberly flopped down on the Ferrari's passenger seat and sighed. "I don't think I took that many pictures for the entire catalog I just finished," she added with a smile in his direction.

"Yeah, it's been a long day." He turned on the ignition and pulled away from the curb.

Kimberly glanced at him from the corner of her eye, unable to understand his sullen mood. Perhaps her family overwhelmed him? Maybe the chaos of all the kids running around overwhelmed him? Her nieces and nephews were a rather rambunctious group when all together. If you weren't accustomed to being around children, they certainly could be an intimidating bunch.

She tried to recall if Jake had ever mentioned having any relatives outside of his brother and grandfather. There were none that she could remember, which meant that Jake probably had never been around small children. Particularly small children who loved to climb all over their aunts and uncles' backs or roll around on the ground tickling each other.

She should have realized how overwhelming her family could be to an outsider. It never occurred to her until now. Kimberly took another glimpse of Jake's profile as they sailed along the freeway, his expression serious and unchanged.

"Jake," she began cautiously when they were almost home. "I'm sorry if the kids were a bit much today. They seemed to be in rare form this afternoon. I only now realized that you're probably not used to being around so many children, and I forgot how troublesome they can appear at times. They really are good kids though," she added with a slight upward tilt of her lips. She absently twirled a long black curl between her forefinger and thumb, as she waited for his reaction.

Jake looked in his rear-view mirror before he changed car lanes in preparation to exit at the ramp to Sunnyvale. He maneuvered the Ferrari off the highway and down the winding ramp, and she continued to wait for his response. He braked slowly for the stoplight at the bottom of the ramp.

"They're all great kids," he finally said. Within seconds the light turned green, and he turned left without looking at her.

"Yeah, I think so too." She was relieved to find that her nieces and nephews were not to blame for his somber mood. Although, that meant something else was to blame, and she worried over what it could be.

"Carly's daughters are quiet, but I think George's daughter more than makes up for them," Jake commented, with the first smile in her direction since getting into the car. Stopped at another traffic light, his hands rested lazily on the steering wheel.

"George's daughter, Maggie, is a talker. That's for sure." A smile quickly formed on her lips. "Sometimes I think Carly and Damien's girls are still adjusting to being part of the family. Lindsay and Samantha have gone through a lot for being only five and six years old. Carly's the only mother they've really known. Damien's first wife took off right after Lindsay was born, and they lived with their grandmother because Damien was always on tour. When Carly and Damien married last year, the girls went to live with them. This past year is the first stability they've really ever known, even with Damien rarely at home."

If Jake caught the edge of bitterness in her voice, he didn't let it show, and she was grateful. She wasn't in the mood to discuss her sister's husband. Her focus was on Jake and the possible reasons for his mood change this afternoon.

"Maggie reminds me of you."

"Well, if she's anything like me, then she will probably grow up wishing for straight hair. I cringe when I think of my poor mother trying to put a brush through my hair every morning. I pray that if I have daughters, they have poker-straight hair." She pushed several curls from her face, and when she turned her head to look at him, she found him staring out the windshield again.

"All six of them." He angled his head toward her, and a lopsided grin played on his lips.

"Six girls! Jake, you're terrible. I wouldn't wish six daughters on anyone."

"Adverse to large families?"

"Not at all. Growing up, I used to tell my parents that I wanted twelve children, six boys, six girls." She chuckled softly. "And that we planned to live with them, forever. My father would respond by saying that he and my mother were going to move while I was in college and not provide me with their forwarding address." She laughed again. "I've resigned myself to the fact that I'll be lucky to have three children. Let's face it, Jake, I'm thirty-one years old."

"Yeah, well, I doubt you'll have any problems. I'm sure you'll make a great mother."

"Thanks."

She glanced at him, and he turned away, but not before she saw the small tick pulsing at the base of his jaw when they pulled into her driveway minutes later.

His emotions had wavered back and forth between sullen and light-hearted for the entire ride home, and she had no idea why. Maybe he was tired? She doubted that was the reason, but desperately wanted to believe it.

They pulled into the garage, and she started to ask him what was wrong when he turned off the engine and practically bolted out of the car. Frustrated, she got out of the car and followed him into the house without a word or a glance exchanged between them.

Chapter 9

Kimberly paced the living room, and debated with herself whether to finally confront him or not. He had been locked up in his room ever since they had come home from George's birthday party, nearly two hours prior. "What could have happened?" she whispered to herself, over and over again. She played back every word they had spoken to each other from the time they left the house this afternoon until the end of the party, three hours later. Nothing. She could come up with nothing to explain Jake's sudden withdrawal from her.

She squared her shoulders and decided to go to his room and confront him. She would use the pretense of being hungry and ask if he wanted to order out for dinner. She took a deep breath and climbed the stairs. She paused in front of his bedroom door. She chewed on her lower lip as she began to have second thoughts. Maybe he was just tired and wanted to catch up on some sleep. Doubtful. It was a lame excuse she wasn't even willing to buy. Frustrated, she muttered a curse she rarely used. She didn't want to come off as clinging and insecure, but his behavior this afternoon left her nerves on edge. She knew she wouldn't relax until she talked to him. She pushed a stray lock of hair to behind her ear and knocked on the door.

"Come in."

She opened the bedroom door and stepped inside with small, hesitant steps. She stood only a few steps inside the doorway and swallowed several times while she waited for him to look up from the book in his hand. Seated in the room's only chair, he looked relaxed and annoyingly preoccupied in his book.

"It's almost eight o'clock, and I wanted to know if you are hungry, if you wanted to order take-out, maybe from that new Chinese restaurant we both want to try?" Her heart pounded wildly in her chest when Jake's eyes roamed over the length of her and eventually settled on her face.

"I don't think so. I'm not really hungry. Thanks, anyway." He continued to watch her, his expression unreadable.

Was she being dismissed? How dare he treat her like this. Anger quickly replaced her earlier apprehension. "Jake, I don't understand. What's going on? What happened between the time we left here this morning and now?"

Jake never hated himself more than he did at this moment. "I don't know what you mean, Kim." He clenched his back teeth together. Although Kimberly's rigid stance said she was ready for battle, her eyes gave her away. She glared at him, but he could still see the hurt reflected in her eyes and the confusion marring her features. He needed to talk to her, to explain. He owed her that much.

He closed his book and placed it on the night stand. He didn't know why he thought he could lose himself in a book anyway. He had barely read two pages during the last hour. He raked his hand through his hair several times before he stood up and crossed the room to stand next to the window. He stared out the pane of glass with his arms crossed in front of his chest. Finally, after several minutes, he turned to face her. He noticed that she still hovered near the door.

"Kim," he began. "Last night was a mistake. I'm sorry. It's my fault. I took advantage of you when you obviously had had too much to drink, and I apologize. I take full responsibility for everything that happened between us." He leaned against the windowsill and patiently waited for her response. He braced himself for her tears, hating himself for being the cause of them.

He was not at all prepared for her reaction. Rage, far worse than he ever thought Kimberly capable of, settled in her deep brown eyes.

She breached the distance between them with angry strides before she stopped to stand less than a foot away from him. She was angrier than he had ever seen her, and she deserved to be. Something wonderful had happened between them, something he had never experienced before in his life, and he knew it had been the same for her. Now he threw it back in her face, as if it meant nothing to him. It had taken everything in him to call last night a mistake, and while he wanted to take the words back, he knew he couldn't.

"You're sorry for last night?" She lashed out. "You take full responsibility?" she hissed mere inches from his face. Her entire body visibly shook with anger, and he wanted nothing than more to call back his lies, but he couldn't. As a couple, they were not meant to be.

"How... how, dare you, Jake Taylor!" Kimberly raised her hand in the air before either of them knew what she planned to do. Her palm collided with the side of his face with a startling intensity. *Smack!*

Kimberly's eyes widened to a point that he thought they might actually pop out of her face. She rubbed her palms together, and he assumed that she experienced something similar to his own pain. She looked him straight in the face, anger expressed in eyes glazed over with unshed tears. "That, Mr. Jake Taylor," she informed him with an arrogant toss of her hair, "was for the apologies you forgot. Specifically, for taking advantage of me at one-thirty in the morning, again at three-thirty, then at five o'clock this morning. And let's not forget your *good morning kiss* at eleven-thirty, followed by a quickie in the shower." She clenched her fists at her sides and turned to walk out of the room.

Jake's hand swiftly left his side to grab her by the arm before she had a chance to take more than a few steps away from him. He grasped her forearm and whirled her around to face him. "Kim," he bit out in a barely controlled whisper, although his own temper was at the bubbling point. "Kim, you don't understand—"

"You're right, I don't understand," she interrupted and yanked her arm out of his grasp. Her brows were narrowed over her dark eyes and her lips curled in distaste. "I don't understand how I could have spent the last twenty years thinking I loved you. I don't understand how I could be such a fool for falling into bed with you because I thought you returned my feelings. I was just someone to warm your bed. For you, I was just one in a long list of easy lays—"

Jake grabbed her other forearm and curled each of his hands around her arms in a deathly grip. "Easy lays? If you think I treated you like some kind of whore, then maybe you better learn the difference." Jake bent his head and captured her lips in a punishing kiss. He coerced her back against the adjacent wall, determined to show her how much her accusation hurt him.

He planted his strong legs in front of her and blocked her escape from his forced embrace. While one of his hand held her head in a bruising kiss, the other hand rapidly traveled under her blouse and over her ribcage. He continued to assault her lips with his own, and he swallowed each of her soft moans. He fumbled for only a second with her bra, before he made quick haste of the center clasp. His hands felt rough against her naked breasts, the slow tenderness of their earlier lovemaking gone.

Kimberly choked out a cry, then went limp, and sagged in his arms. She no longer participated in their impassioned lovemaking, and it was as if a bucket of ice water had been thrown over his head. He swore under his breath. What the hell was he doing? He only meant to frighten her, to get back at her for thinking that when he made love to her, it meant nothing to him. *My God, what have I done?* He backed away from her, his face devoid of color. He ran shaky fingers through his hair, positive now that he had lost his mind. "Kim, I... I'm sorry." He took several ragged breaths. "I only meant to show you...hell, I'm so sorry."

He walked over to bed and sat down on the edge of the mattress. He rested his elbows against his knees and buried his head in his hands. He didn't understand how he could have gotten so carried away. Never before in his life had he let himself get so out of control with a woman. He had to leave, had to get away from her before he harmed her any further. He lifted his head, intent on getting up when she sat down beside him.

"Jake," she whispered brokenly. She walked over to the bed and sat down next to him. "Jake, I love you. Please tell me what's wrong. Please."

Jake looked into her eyes, brimmed with tears. After the way he had just treated her, she responded with *I love you*? He shook his head in disgust. He didn't deserve her, never would, but he needed to tell her the truth. She deserved at least that much from him. "Shh, Kim. Please don't talk about love, not with me."

He reached over and wiped a sole tear off of her cheek with the tip of his finger. He breathed deeply before beginning, "Kim, I don't know how much you know about my marriage or divorce, so I'm going to start from the beginning." He placed a soft kiss on her forehead before he stood up and walked over to the window. He was on the brink of conjuring up all of the ugly memories from the past, and he didn't want to be near Kimberly while he did it. He knew she would be able to see past his cold words into the pain that was nestled in his heart. She would offer her sympathy, and he would be all too willing to accept it. And he couldn't. Kimberly deserved someone a hell of a lot better than him, and he would make sure that she understood just that.

"Kimberly, when I was thirteen, I got mumps. A severe case. We... Zane, Gramps, and I," he clarified, "had just moved to California. Fortunately, Zane was at baseball camp when I first broke out, so he was spared from getting infected. Anyway, Gramps took me to a doctor, who basically suggested I take some aspirin and get a lot of rest. Gramps believed that if we had still been in Texas, and I had seen our family doctor, my case of the mumps might not have become so severe. Even though he called our doctor in Texas, and was told that wasn't necessarily the case, Gramps still felt responsible."

Kimberly stared back at him, confusion radiated from her eyes. "Jake, I don't understand? Weren't you vaccinated? I thought all kids were vaccinated for mumps."

Jake sighed. "My grandfather thought I had been, so he contacted the pediatrician my mother had taken us to as kids and was told that according to their records, my mother had refused to get us vaccinated. She had had this idea that they did more harm than good. My grandfather had no idea. Everyone, including our new doctors, assumed we had been vaccinated. I don't think my grandfather ever forgave her." He ran a hand over his chin. "As soon as I was better, and Zane was back from camp, Gramps made sure our vaccines were up to date."

"I still don't understand."

"Kim." He slowly turned to confront her. "I had a severe case of mumps as a teenage boy. I developed Orchitis, which is an inflammation of the, well, I'm not going to go into the details. Let's just say it was bad and extremely unpleasant." Jake shifted his stance to look out the window again. He shook his head, and his laughter was filled with bitterness. "It left me sterile. I can't have children."

He waited for her gasp of shock, and even though he was surprised when it never came, he continued. "I met Brenda soon after graduate school. I was up front about my inability to 'reproduce' right from the beginning. Brenda's reaction was different from any other girl I dated. She was elated. She joked about how lucky it was that she would never have to worry about birth control. She was a dedicated career girl, she had told me. She had no room in her life, then or in the future, for children. We married a year after we met. Neither of us had much family, so it was a simple ceremony by a Justice of the Peace in Boston."

He stared at the floor. "Soon after we got married, I landed a job as a journalist for a major network. I began traveling all over the world. Brenda was an interior designer, which I mistakenly thought kept her occupied while I was away. I was making pretty good money, considering my lack of experience and age at the time. When Brenda suggested we buy a house in the suburbs of New York, complete with four bedrooms and a big backyard, I didn't even protest. I felt so guilty for leaving her alone while I was off on assignments that I indulged her any time the opportunity presented itself. Brenda had been having a hard time with her own career and decided to take time off to evaluate what she wanted to do with her life."

"One night, when we had been married almost two years, we went to dinner at a neighbor's house. I think their names were Cynthia and Bill or Bob, something like that. I barely knew them, but apparently Brenda had become rather close to Cynthia. Her husband also traveled a lot as a salesman, and she stayed at home with their three children. I knew within minutes after we walked through their front door that Brenda had changed her mind about having children. The signs were there before she met Cynthia, but I guess I pretended to believe otherwise. It finally dawned on me that night that we owned a four-bedroom house, and I had no idea why." Jake paused and thought that he might take a walk tonight, maybe it would help ease the headache that pounded harder as the day progressed. He shook his head and turned to stare out the window to see a pair of teenagers kissing underneath the street light.

Jake turned around and forced himself to continue, "I confronted Brenda as soon as we returned home. She confessed that she had had a change of heart and wanted children. She pleaded with me to have some tests taken and to consult some specialists about my problem."

"I refused because I knew it was hopeless. I thought the discussion was closed, but that wasn't the case. Brenda decided to take a more overt approach. She bought every book, magazine, and pamphlet ever written on the subjects of sterility and infertility. She became obsessed, forwarding articles to my email and begging me to read them. She left books in the bathroom, stuck them in my suitcase, and left them next to the remote control. I couldn't open a drawer in the house without the word infertility staring me in the face. She contacted specialists all over the country and arranged for them to call me directly."

Jake ran his fingers along his neck, and his hand stopped to massage the tense muscles at the back of his neck. "It got to the point that I couldn't wait for my next assignment. About the time I thought I had neared the point of insanity, I met a journalist who told me about two children he adopted from Guatemala. I was ecstatic. Adoption. Why hadn't I thought of that before?"

"Brenda was mortified." He shook his head as he recalled her outraged reaction. "Adoption? How ridiculous, she told me at the time. She would never consider adoption, not when she was perfectly capable of having children, she told me. And I, she claimed, denied her the opportunity. Soon everything became my fault. I was selfish. I was insensitive. I didn't care."

"Brenda became obsessed with having my sterility problem cured. She became more enraged each time that I refused to be tested. She started creating scenes when we were in public. She complained to complete strangers how selfish her husband was and how he denied her the children she desperately wanted."

Jake took a deep, ragged breath as he recalled the next ugly memory. "On Christmas day--we had been married over three years by this time-- we went to my sister-in-law's house. Karen, Brenda's sister, had divorced before her daughter Alicia was born. Alicia was adorable at three-years-old and took to me right away. I was reading her some book, I don't know, 'Dora the Doctor' or something like that, and Alicia was sitting on my lap. Brenda walked in on us and she, ah, she freaked out. She demanded that I stay away from her niece since I hated children. She acted as if I was a child molester or something."

"I should have confronted her about our situation before then." He exhaled deeply. "I had avoided it and the possibility of divorce. My own parents had never married, and I just didn't want to go there, I guess." His shoulders slumped, and he gazed out window, consumed by his memories.

"Soon after our visit to Karen's house, Brenda started to accuse me of disliking children. I secretly hated children, Brenda would tell me over breakfast. Or

126

the topic of conversation at dinner would be how jealous I was of all the attention a child would demand."

Jake turned around to look at Kimberly, still seated quietly on the bed. "Our final argument, ironically, was after we returned home from a trip out west and attended one of your brother's Fourth of July parties.

"We argued, rather brutally, neither of us holding anything back. I went out for a walk afterwards, and when I returned home several hours later, poof!... Brenda was gone, along with all of our savings and anything of value in the house. End of marriage. End of story." He moved his bottom jaw back and forth and pressed his lips together. Her rejection still hurt, dammit. Despite everything, it still hurt.

He wanted to go outside for some air and was about to, when Kimberly walked over to stand in front of him. "Jake, I'm so sorry, but not every woman is like Brenda. I'm not like Brenda. Jake, things will be different between us—"

"No, you don't understand. I don't want there to be an us. I don't want an us with anyone. I went through hell with Brenda, and I won't do it again—"

"But—"

"Don't bother, Kimberly. I heard it all before from Brenda. 'Kids aren't important. We have each other, blah, blah, blah.' Kim, I don't want the family thing anymore. I'll be thirty-five years old next month. I'm set in my career, and I want different things out of my life now." He tilted his head and looked her directly in the eyes before he continued. "Kim, I don't love you. I like you. I respect you." *I love you more than I thought possible to love anyone,* he silently added. He realized with a startling intensity that he loved her, and that was why, above everything else, he had to make her understand that she needed to get on with her life without him. Someday, she would meet and marry a man who deserved her, and they would have all the children she ever dreamed of. She would forget about Jake Taylor.

"I like my life the way it is, Kimberly. I see the world. Each day is a different challenge." *I'd give anything to wake up next to you every morning. I wouldn't care if I ever traveled outside of San Francisco again if I could only be with you.* Jake swallowed back the hard lump in his throat. He lifted her chin up with his thumb. He watched her swipe at the tears that spilled out of the corners of her wide, dark eyes, and it broke his heart. "Kimberly, you'll always be special to me."

"Thanks, a lot," she whispered. She tore her chin from his grasp and stepped away from him. She pushed her shoulders back and tilted her head proudly as she walked toward the bedroom door. Before she stepped through the doorway, she paused. He watched her clench her hands at her side before she turned around to glare at him. "I hope your suitcase keeps you warm at night, Jake. And that it's there for you during the holidays, or when you're sick, or when you're too old to travel... I would have stuck by you through anything, Jake Taylor. But instead, you decided to break my heart. I would like to break yours in return, but obviously you don't have one."

Jake felt the slam of her bedroom door shake the entire second floor. "Damn," he swore quietly and proceeded to punch his fist against the bedroom wall. He leaned his forehead on the wall. His arm rested above his head to brace his body. "Damn," he repeated.

Chapter 10

"Hello?" Kimberly asked groggily. She cradled the cell between her shoulder and ear while she struggled to untangle herself from the bed sheets. She pushed several strands of hair from her face, as she forced herself to keep from yawning into the receiver.

"Yes, this is Kimberly Urbane." She held her hand over the mouthpiece to conceal the yawn she finally allowed to escape.

"What?" She sat up in bed, now fully awake.

"Paris? Milan? Today? Paris?" she repeated in an effort to try and think straight. What do I do? Her magazine editor needed her to cover runway shows in Paris and a magazine spread in Milan. She looked across her room into the mirror above her dresser. Crying half of the night had left her eyes swollen and with traces of mascara smeared beneath them.

"What? Yes, I'm still here. I'm sorry. I'm trying to recall my schedule for the next two weeks. It's so last minute... yes, I realize you're in a bind. Ah, ah, please give me a minute to think." Kimberly gazed again at her reflection in the mirror. The aftermath of her argument with Jake the night before was evident in the dark circles under her eyes.

She felt as if she had gone through a war and lost. In a sense, she had. She heard Jake's voice echo through her head, *"Kim, I don't love you."* She pushed back the pain that surfaced again in her heart, and she knew what her decision had to be. "I'll do it," she responded before she changed her mind.

"Yes, I can be ready in three hours. Thanks." She disconnected the call in a daze. She had just received the opportunity of a lifetime for a fashion photographer, so where was the feeling of elation that was supposed to be overwhelming her? Where was the sensation of having 'arrived' in the world of fashion photography? It was non-existent, non-existent because she realized that she would rather stay at home with Jake than further her career in the photography world. Even though he may not love her, that didn't mean her own feelings had changed overnight. She groaned as she got out of bed. She had a lot of things to do to get ready for her trip and only three hours before a car arrived to take her to the airport.

Two and half hours later, she carried her suitcases down the stairs, while she mentally ran through her checklist again to ensure she had packed everything she needed. She glanced at the thin gold watch on her wrist and decided that if she had forgotten anything, she would just have to buy it in Paris. It would bust her monthly budget if she spent over two hundred dollars, but she hadn't been thinking clearly when she packed, and she knew that it was likely that something had been forgotten.

"Where is Jake?" She peered out the front door and down the street. The car arranged for her by the magazine was due at the house in thirty minutes, and neither Jake, nor Daisy, were anywhere to be found.

When she had found Daisy missing earlier that morning, she had assumed that Daisy was with Jake and not roaming the streets, and now she realized that she should have confirmed it. She checked behind the back of the closet door and saw that the dog's leash was gone. That was as good of an indication as any that Jake had taken Daisy out for a walk. The fact that he had been gone long enough to walk the large St. Bernard to Los

Angeles did not sit well with her. Jake and Daisy had been gone by the time she went downstairs to fix her first cup of coffee for the morning, and that had been two hours ago. He hadn't left a note, nor had he answered any of her text messages.

Kimberly checked her watch again. She was on the verge of panic, when the back door opened. She whirled around at the sound and ran into the kitchen. "Jake, I'm glad you're finally back. Where's Daisy?"

"I left her out back. Her paws are muddy from our excursion in the park. I need to give her a bath." His eyes reflected his surprise to find her speaking to him this morning, and they both knew it. If he was surprised now, wait until she told him about her trip. She clasped her hands together and found her palms were damp.

"Kim, what's going on?"

Kimberly wondered if he had slept at all last night, or if the sound of her weeping throughout the night had kept him awake. She had tried to bury her sobs in her pillow, but the walls were thin, and there were times during the night that her heartbreak had overwhelmed her.

"Jake, you're not going to believe it!" She forced her lips upward into a dazzling smile. How a fashion model could plaster a fake smile on her face for the cameras, sometimes for sixteen hours a day, was beyond Kim's comprehension. One minute of the false pretense, and she wanted to let her lips sag into the deep scowl she had been wearing all morning. "My magazine editor called this morning while you were out with Daisy. She wants me to photograph some runway shows for the magazine, followed by some magazine spreads. One week in Paris and the next in Milan." She straightened her shoulders and forced herself to continue with her explanation. If she paused even for a minute, she wouldn't be able to continue her pretend enthusiasm for the upcoming assignment.

"According to my editor, the photographer assigned to the project broke her leg skiing in Tahoe over the weekend and failed to call the magazine until this morning."

"I see," Jake responded as if he understood, although his eyes reflected something altogether different. "Isn't this rather short notice?"

"Of course, it is Jake. But Paris and Milan? I may never have a chance like this again." At least I hope I don't. Paris, the City of Love? Of all places she could be going to after last night, it had to be one of the most romantic cities in the world. And Milan wasn't much better. She would much rather stay at home, mope around the house, and pour her heart out to Daisy than fly anywhere. The dog was as good of a listener as any, and she certainly didn't blab everything people told her. Kim sighed despairingly. "Daisy! Jake, I forgot about Daisy. I mean, if you wouldn't mind, ah, do you think you could take care of her for me? I know it's a lot to ask and if it's too much trouble, I can always call Carly—"

"Kim, it's fine," he interrupted and reassured her with a small smile. "I, I'm just having a hard time trying to understand why you took this assignment in the first place? You told me you don't like doing runway shows."

"I said that? Well, I guess I changed my mind." She diverted her eyes to a place somewhere over his shoulder.

"I don't think so," Jake returned bluntly. "I think you took this job because of what happened between us last night. And if that's the case Kim, don't do it. I'll leave. I can get a hotel room if you don't want to be around me—"

"Jake, don't be ridiculous." She laughed a bit too harshly for it to be genuine. She walked over to the refrigerator and took out a Coke to avoid looking at him. "Last night has nothing to do with me taking this assignment. I've just received the opportunity to cover several Ready-to-Wear runway shows in Paris and a magazine shoot in Milan. Ready-to-Wear is the big time for fashion. Top designers from all over the world will be presenting their lines, most of it mass merchandised throughout the world, and I'm going to be right in the middle of it taking pictures for one of the top fashion magazines in the country." She took her time pouring the soft drink into her glass, anything to avoid facing him.

"This is an opportunity of a lifetime for me, Jake." She shrugged and took a sip of her drink. "I wouldn't miss it for the world." It took every ounce of pride she contained in her 5' 10" frame to keep from refuting her own lie. She had to do this. She didn't have a choice. Jake didn't love her, and somehow, she had to learn to deal with that cold, hard fact, even though her heart wanted to crumble into a million pieces because of it.

"Can I drive you to the airport?"

She glanced out the kitchen window. "No thanks, the magazine arranged a car for me."

"Okay."

She glanced back at him, and he stood near the back door in silence. He stared at her, and she squirmed under his intense scrutiny. He appeared to accept her decision, and all she could do was wish that he would beg her to stay. Her heart crumbled a little more. If only he would tell her that he had been lying, that he did love her and everything would be alright between them. She looked into the hazel eyes she had dreamed of gazing into for the rest of her life and realized he wouldn't tell her the words she needed to hear. Not now, not ever.

"I better get going. The driver should be here any minute." She placed her glass in the sink and hurried out of the kitchen. She grabbed her purse and cellphone on the way out, and Jake followed closely behind her.

After the limo driver placed her suitcases in the trunk, he returned to his seat behind the steering wheel, and Jake and Kimberly were left to stand alone on the curb. "I left my itinerary on a piece of paper stuck to the refrigerator, in case you need to track me down and I don't answer my cellphone because I forgot to charge it." She knew they were both thinking about the last time she hadn't answered her cellphone, and he had confronted her in the kitchen. "I think there is enough dog food in the pantry, so Daisy should be all right. I can't think of anything else, unless I forgot to pay the electric bill. I guess you'll know when you come home and the lights don't work." She smiled hesitantly at him.

"Don't worry, Daisy and I will be fine."

More than anything in the world, she wanted him to reach out and pull her into his embrace. She yearned for him to take her lips under his own, to have his arms hold her tightly against him. She searched his eyes, and she swore she saw the pain she experienced reflected in his face. She waited for him to make a move toward her, and when he didn't, the agony of his rejection shot through her like a jolt to her soul.

"Text me when you arrive so I know you made it okay?" he asked her after a lengthy silence, even though he had to know she wouldn't do it. Any communication, even to ask for updates on Daisy's welfare, would be too much for her. He had broken her heart last night and had reinforced the break again by his indifference this morning. No, she wouldn't be texting him from Paris.

"Sure." She forced herself to smile at him. "I, ah, better get going, the driver is waiting," she pointed out with a nod of her head in the direction of the limo's front seat.

"Yeah. Well, take care of yourself."

He had to know he was a fool for allowing their relationship to deteriorate to this point, but he couldn't see it any other way, and he refused to listen to her. There was nothing else for her to do but leave. "Yeah, I'll see you." She pressed her lips into a tiny smile and turned away. She allowed him to open the car door for her, and she murmured her gratitude, as he closed it once she was inside. She knew he expected her to roll down the window and wave goodbye, but she couldn't. Instead she faced forward and alerted the driver that she was ready. As the driver shifted the car into gear, she forced herself to refrain from looking out of the side window. Relief poured through her when she felt the car pull away from the curb, and she was finally able to release the tears she had held until now.

*****

Jake stood on the sidewalk and stared in the direction of the limo long after it disappeared from sight. Maybe her leaving wouldn't be such a bad thing after all. They both needed time apart from each other, and two weeks was a starting point. Hopefully, Kimberly would use the time to realize that it would have never worked between them. She would come to the same realization he had at George's party. Children were a vital and important part of her life, one she wouldn't want to miss out on.

As for himself, he could use the time to push aside the feelings of loneliness and despair that engulfed him. He had done it before, and he could do it again. He sighed, sure he could. He kicked a pebble on the sidewalk with his foot. He would give Daisy a bath and then visit his grandfather. "My grandfather might not be doing too well lately, but hell, neither am I," he muttered to himself. "We make a perfect pair."

Chapter 11

"Hello, Mr. Taylor," the nurse greeted him upon his exit from the elevator on his grandfather's floor.

"Hi." Jake signed the guest registry, while the nurse updated him on his grandfather's status.

"He's been asleep all day again today. The doctor was in to see him this morning, and as before, he says that your grandfather is not in any pain. They're going to try to switch his medication to see if that makes a difference. His heart is strong, as you know, and everything else seems to be in good working condition. Since he stopped participating in physical therapy, he is too tired to do much else than stay awake for his meals." The nurse paused while she waited for Jake to finish signing the registry. "Based on the stories he told us when he first arrived, your grandfather has had a good life," she added with a sympathetic smile.

"Yeah, he has." He nodded and then handed the nurse her pen and walked away.

Jake stepped into his grandfather's room, and a wave of sadness overwhelmed him, much as it had over the past week. His strong, ornery grandfather lay listlessly in bed, his only movement the rise and fall of his broad chest. His hair lay in thick waves as it had most of his eighty-five years. A thousand tiny wrinkles crisscrossed the old man's skin, each a reminder of the burning Houston sun he had spent so many years working under.

Jake felt a large lump form in his throat, as he pulled a chair next to his grandfather's bed. There were so many things he still wanted to tell his grandfather. Grandpa Zack had always been there for him, ready to help him out and lend some advice when he thought Jake needed it. "What am I going to do without you, Gramps?" Jake placed his grandfather's thin, weathered hand in his own.

He closed his hand over his grandfather's and willed him to live. For several minutes Jake held Gramps' hand in silence, unable to put into words what he wanted to say to him.

He pressed his eyes closed and swallowed back the lump in his throat. Finally, he took a deep breath and opened his eyes. "Gramps," he began in a low voice. "I... I hope you can hear me, because I need to talk to you. Why I've saved everything up inside me until now, I can't say. I only hope that you can forgive me for never telling you sooner."

"You see, Gramps. You're the only real parent I've ever had. Mom died so long ago that I barely have any memory of her. You've been both my mother and father all these years, and I can't imagine life without you. I mean who else would have encouraged a kid who never played an organized sport in his life to try out for a big city high school football team his first year at a new school? Or loaned me his car so I could go carousing with my friends and then said nothing when I returned it with a dent in the front bumper? Or convinced me to try my hand at journalism, even though you harass me about now and I know you don't mean it, when all the other kids went into business or medicine at college? You, Gramps, you. You've always been there for me."

Jake took another deep breath, that damn lump in his throat just wouldn't go away. "I know you've carried the guilt around about me getting mumps, but it was inevitable. Houston or San Francisco, it wouldn't have mattered. You had no control over me getting the mumps; nobody did, except my mom, and well, she must have thought she was doing the right thing at the time. Please always believe that, Gramps. I do." Jake smoothed his thumb over the skin on his grandfather's palm and was reminded of how hard the thin, wrinkled hand had worked for so many years.

"Gramps, I need to talk to you about Kimberly." He swiped away a wisp of hair that lay against his grandfather's forehead, close to his eyes. "I know you would have liked to have seen us get together... but it's not going to happen. I've caught every hint you've dropped these past weeks, and it just won't work. I, I'm not what Kimberly needs. Gramps, you even call me a hippie with my long hair and wandering ways. Kimberly wouldn't want someone like that. I mean, I'm gone for months at a time, sometimes not even able to get cell reception for days. What kind of a life is that?" He paused, his eyes flickered over his grandfather's still form.

"Gramps, who am I trying to kid? You know as well as I do why it would never work between Kimberly and me. If you could have seen her face at George's birthday party, Gramps. Her beautiful brown eyes light up when she holds a baby in her arms. Kids adore her, and she adores them. She deserves better than me. She's beautiful, she's intelligent, and she's witty. She'll find someone to fill up her heart and forget I ever existed." Jake leaned his elbows on the edge of his grandfather's bed railing. He lowered his forehead to his hands, his grandfather's hand still held tightly in his grasp.

"Gramps, I know what you would say right now and you're right. I've... I've fallen in love with her. But don't you see? Brenda's rejection nearly destroyed me. A life spent with Kimberly would be a prison sentence for both of us. She claims she loves me, but I would never be completely sure. I'd always wonder if she was happy, if she regretted her decision not to have children. I couldn't do it, Gramps, not to Kimberly, not to myself," he choked out, his voice deep and husky with emotion.

Jake sat for several minutes in silence. There was so much more he wanted to say, but he was talked out. Emotionally spent. All other confessions would have to wait for another day. He remained hunched over his grandfather's bed deep in thought and oblivious to the passing of time. Minutes or perhaps hours later, the door opened, and he brought his head up from the pillow he had created out of his and his grandfather's hands.

"Excuse me." The nurse's voice echoed against the walls of the plain room. "But visiting hours are over, Mr. Taylor, and it's time for your grandfather's medicine." The nurse waited patiently for him to respond, a smile of understanding plastered on her pleasant face.

"Sure. I must have lost track of time." Jake rose from the side of the bed. He wiped away the excess moisture at the corner of his eyes and then pushed his hair behind his ears.

Jake glanced at the nurse and then back at his grandfather. He bent down over his grandfather and placed a kiss on the old man's forehead. "I love you, Gramps." He clenched his grandfather's hand one last time, and as he did, his heartbeat quickened when he felt his grandfather squeeze his hand back. He turned his head toward the nurse, and she returned his gaze with a small smile on her lips.

Reluctantly, Jake let go of his grandfather's hand and returned his chair back to the corner of the room. He paused at the doorway to look at his grandfather one last time, before he walked out of the room.

****

Jake held onto the house keys with one hand and the doorknob with the other when his cellphone began to ring. "Hello?" He pushed the door opened and walked into the house.

"Yes, this is Jake Taylor." Daisy ran to his side, and he automatically reached out and scratched the top of her head.

"No. I was just there, less than a half an hour ago. He squeezed my hand. I know he did."

He brushed his hand across his jaw and took a deep breath. "No, I think I'd rather come back tonight and take care of things. Thank you." Jake disconnected the call and afterwards sat down on the living room couch in little more than a daze. He willed himself to release the myriad of emotions that welled up inside of him. It didn't work. He felt cold, dead inside, unable to feel anything.

He stood up and mentally prepared himself to return to the rehab center. He had lost both Kimberly and his grandfather in less than two weeks. He felt numb inside, beyond feeling anymore. He thought he had understood what it meant to be lonely. He laughed bitterly. He never knew what loneliness meant, not until now.

Chapter 12

Kimberly fumbled with her key ring when the front door opened without her assistance. Arms laden with several bags, her head popped up from the doorknob to look straight into Jake's eyes. "Jake, thanks," she breathed a sigh of relief.

"It's four-thirty in the morning. What on earth are you doing awake?" Between the two of them, they managed to carry all of her luggage into the house in one trip. "Just put my stuff at the bottom of the stairs. I'll bring it up later," she called out.

Kimberly shook off her light fall coat, prepared to hang it over the back of a chair in the living room rather than hang it up in the closet because she was that tired. She stopped mid-step when she spotted a suitcase in the doorway of the living room. "Jake?" She flung her coat carelessly onto the floor.

"Jake?" she repeated as she walked down the hallway toward the coat closet. "Jake, what's going on?" She watched him put on his leather jacket, before he stuffed his wallet into an inside breast pocket.

"Jake, are you going to answer me?" She began to tremble inside and out. When he continued to avoid eye contact with her, the reality of the situation finally dawned on her. She brought her hand over her mouth to squelch the sob that formed in her throat.

Jake tilted his head to look at her, and his hazel eyes bore into her despite the dimly lit room. "I have a flight to Saudi Arabia this morning, Kim. I booked it after I received your text from Milan yesterday. I waited for you to come home to tell you and to make sure you were home for Daisy."

"My flight was delayed. I sent you a text. I was supposed to be home several hours ago," she whispered in a dazed tone. "Please, Jake. Don't do this. Don't leave. Listen to me." A cold, sense of loss flowed through her, and it chilled her to the bone. "I did a lot of thinking while I was away. Jake, I was wrong to want more from you than you are willing to give. I know that now. Jake, please. November is a long way off. You have almost a month before you promised to return to the Middle East. Jake, please. I'm sorry, can't you see that? Please don't leave because of my foolishness." She breached the gap between them and tenderly reached out to place her hand on his forearm. He flinched and took a step back from her.

"Jake? What have I done that is so terrible that you can't stand my touch?" This was her fault. If she hadn't been such a child and run away from him when she had... perhaps if she would have stayed and proven that she needed only him, his bag wouldn't be packed and sitting in the hall. His leaving had been her own doing. She had no one to blame but herself. She had given him two weeks to realize how selfish and immature she was, and he had apparently taken full advantage of the time.

Defeated in more ways than she ever dreamed possible, Kimberly looked him straight in the eyes. "Have a nice trip," she murmured and then turned away from him. She was determined to go upstairs to her room and sleep for a week. Hopefully by then, the ugly nightmare she found herself in would be over. She neared the doorway when Jake wrapped his hand around her wrist and twisted her to him.

"Kim." He dragged his fingers through the hair at the side of his head. "I'm leaving because I no longer have a reason for being here."

"What?" She studied his handsome face and noticed the small lines around the corner of his eyes that she could have sworn didn't exist two weeks ago. His shoulder length hair was pulled back to the base of his neck, and the style emphasized the tired lines along his forehead. He looked exhausted and something else. She couldn't put her finger on it. Beaten? Defeated? She knew the look well and had worn it herself over the last two weeks, but she never expected to see it on him. She continued to stare at him. Her heartbeat throbbed in her ears as she waited for his explanation.

"My grandfather died, Kim. While you were away." He let out a weary sigh.

"What?" Kimberly whispered and then repeated herself in a near shout. "What? Why didn't you get in contact with me? How could you not tell me, Jake?" She walked over to the couch and threw herself down on it. Grandpa Zack was dead, and Jake hadn't even bothered to reach out to her. "You couldn't even send me a text. Damn you, Jake Taylor, for not telling me."

Jake ran the palm of his hand over his eyes. He sighed in a sound similar to self-disgust, and it echoed throughout the room. He walked over to Kimberly and sat down next to her on the couch. He breathed deeply, and he rubbed his eyes again. "Kim," he began in a consoling tone. "Gramps died about a week after you left. I didn't call you because I knew you would come home. This was your big opportunity. You said so yourself—"

"Grandpa Zack is more important to me, and so are you. I would have wanted to be there for you, Jake, to at least have had the choice." The irony, that she cared nothing about the job she had just completed, did not escape her. She had lied to him, and the lie had cost her the chance to say goodbye to a man she had come to love and respect over the last several weeks.

"I appreciate it, Kim. I do." His voice was a soft caress on her skin, and she felt the effect of it down to the tips of her toes. "If it makes any difference, we didn't have any type of service. Zane came home from the Philippines, and the two of us arranged for his burial. That's all. That's what he wanted." Jake started to reach over and brush a fallen lock of hair from her face but stopped his hand in midair. Instead, he clenched his hands together in his lap. Kimberly didn't miss the gesture and assumed that it was out of habit rather than desire, because in few hours he would board a plane, and he gave her no indication that she could persuade him otherwise.

Somewhat consoled by his explanation and because she knew she was to blame, Kimberly's anger subsided. Unfortunately, she was still left with the fact that he planned to leave, something that she was not prepared to handle after her lonely, tiresome trip. "Jake, this doesn't mean you have to leave. You promised your producer you would return in November. That's still a few weeks away."

"Ah, Kim," he replied brokenly. "You know as well as I do, that I need to leave. We both need to get on with our lives, and it will only make it harder by my staying." Jake pushed up the sleeve of his leather coat and glanced at his watch. "I better get going."

Something snapped inside of Kimberly. Her world had just crashed around her, and she suddenly felt helpless to stop it, but she knew she had to try. "No." She grasped each of his forearms. "Please, Jake. I need you. We can make it together. I know what I said before, no commitments. But, Jake, don't you see? We can make it. I love you, Jake. I've loved you forever. The past two weeks were torture for me. I never stopped thinking about you," She tightened her grasp on his arms, hysteria bubbled up inside of her. "Jake, I don't need children, only you. Please believe that. Jake, please don't leave me, please."

"Kim, please don't do this to me. Not now." He shook his head, removed her hands from her arms, and backed out of her reach. "No." Jake nearly shouted in his defense.

"Kim, I have to go," he choked out in a tortured voice. "Please, Kim, don't do this. Look, I care about you. We'll always be friends—"

"Friends?... Friends? You're not my friend, Jake. My friends don't rip out my heart and then leave me to deal with the damage. No, we can't be friends." She curled herself up into a tight ball with her head rested on top of her knees. "Please go." Her voice trembled, as she swiped the corners of her eyes with the palm of her hand.

"I'm sorry, Kim." Jake whispered and smoothed his hand along the dark hair at the top of her head.

"Please go," she repeated and swatted his hand away from her. She visibly winced when he complied with her demand and stood up. He planned to walk away from her. For good. He thought he had no other choice, and Kimberly was at a loss to convince him otherwise.

She stared longingly at him, unable to stop herself. Maybe she could use the memory of his leaving as a reminder of how he hadn't cared enough to stay and fight for them, when she lay awake at night, foolishly yearning for him.

"Take care of yourself." He waited patiently for her response, but she refused to give him one.

Tears continued to stream down her cheeks, but she remained silent. Finally, he turned and walked away. He reached the edge of the room when she called out to him, her voice rough and raspy from crying.

"Jake?"

"Yes?"

"Goodbye."

Jake visibly winced. His shoulders sagged, and his eyes widened before they became hooded and downcast. Without even a nod of his head, he turned and walked out of the room. Kimberly waited for the sound of the front door to close, and then she buried her head into her hands and wept.

Chapter 13

"I'm coming," Kimberly called from the top of the stairwell. She wiped developing solution on the pant leg of her faded denim coveralls and then pushed her dark rimmed glasses to the top of her head. "Just a minute," she added as she rushed to unlock the front door.

"Carly. Hi."

"Hi. Lindsay and Samantha have a birthday party this afternoon. I dropped them off, and I thought since I was in the neighborhood, I would stop in to see you," Carly explained cheerfully, although Kimberly didn't fail to notice that she avoided eye contact.

Kimberly placed a hand on each of her hips. She didn't buy her sister's story for a minute. "Are you saying the girls are attending a party in my neighborhood, Carly? Forty-five minutes from home? The schools really must be busing children all over the place if your daughters know children who live around here. And where's the baby?" Kimberly raised a challenging eyebrow toward her younger sister. She planned to bar Carly's entrance into the house until she confessed the real reason for her unexpected visit.

"Fine, you win. But I didn't exactly say I dropped them off in your neighborhood. I said that I dropped them off and then was in your neighborhood." Carly took in her unbending stance and in typical Carly fashion, refused to be unnerved by it. "Let me in. It's raining out here. Besides, can't a sister drop in on her sister without her motives being challenged?" Carly huffed and brushed past Kimberly on her way into the hallway. She removed her jacket and hung it up in the closet before she gave Kimberly a chance to protest.

"If a sister is a normal sister, maybe. But, you're not, nor do you ever do anything on a whim. You always have a motive. What is it this time? What harebrained scheme are you going to try to get me to go along with today?" Kimberly probed, not feeling a bit of remorse for giving her sister the third degree. She left one hand on her hip, as she repeatedly tapped the tip of her shoe on the floor, a habit she knew annoyed Carly.

"Kimberly, I am not up to anything. The girls really are at a birthday party this afternoon, and Damien is with the baby. I had a couple of hours to kill. That's all. I came by to see how you are because we haven't seen you lately," she justified with a tilt of her chin.

"I've been busy. I've taken on a lot of freelance work the last two months. You caught me in the middle of developing some pictures I need to send out tomorrow morning, and I'm not nearly done." She'd be daft to think Carly would take the hint, but at least it was worth the try. Resigned to the idea that her sister was not turning around and leaving, she decided to offer her something to drink. "Can I get you a cup of coffee?"

"That sounds wonderful," Carly beamed and followed Kimberly into the kitchen. "You know, the girls were terribly disappointed when you didn't show up for Thanksgiving. You should have seen them. Lindsay dressed up as an Indian Princess, and Samantha was a Pilgrim."

"Yes, well, I'm sure they were adorable, and I'm sorry I couldn't make it, but I had an assignment I had to finish." Plus, I just couldn't face any more questions about Jake, she added to herself. She still felt the pain of his leaving almost eight weeks earlier. She turned on the coffeepot and took out two cups from the cabinet.

"Kimberly!" Carly screeched and nearly caused Kimberly to drop the cups from her hands.

"What is it?" Kimberly whipped around to look at her sister. The way Carly startled her, she better be looking at a spider the size of a small dog.

"Kimberly, why don't you tell me what's really going on here? Look at you. How much weight have you lost? Ten pounds? Fifteen? Kimberly, you're all skin and bones. I didn't notice when I walked in but seeing you here in the kitchen where there's more light, Kimberly, you look terrible. This is my fault, isn't it? If I hadn't pushed Jake and you together, you wouldn't be here, wasting away to nothing," Carly cried dramatically.

Kimberly's eyes traveled over her sister. She took in her perfectly coifed blonde hair, set in a coil at the back of her head. Her fingernails, painted fire hydrant red, were all the same length and not a broken one amongst them. She shook her head. Her beautiful sister had to have more things to do with her time than pry into other peoples' lives. Especially when, nine times out of ten, Carly assumptions came so close to the truth. She had been miserable since Jake left, but she needed to work it out for herself. Jake wasn't coming back, and with time, she would adjust to the idea. Yeah, right.

"Carly, you are not to blame for anything. I told you. I've been working a lot of hours lately. I haven't been eating right the last couple of weeks." Actually, her appetite was all but non-existent. The thought of food nauseated her more times than not, but she certainly would not share that with her sister.

"Jake has nothing to do with it." She turned her attention to the coffee maker after choking out the lie.

"I don't have any cream. Is milk okay?"

"Sure," Carly answered distractedly. Kimberly felt a flush crawl up her cheeks when she opened the refrigerator door, and she hoped Carly missed it. If Carly thought she was still depressed over Jake's leaving, she would demand that they discuss it.

Kimberly placed the milk on the kitchen table, along with a can of Coke for herself. "I feel warm all of a sudden." She made her way to a kitchen chair and sat down. She pressed the cold soft drink against the side of her cheek. The cool metal felt good against her skin. Her body cooled off almost immediately.

"Kimberly, your face is flushed all of a sudden. Are you sure you are all right? Do you think you have the flu? I heard it's going around," Carly added with growing concern.

Kimberly raised her hand and pressed it to the side of her face. She'd welcome the warm flush if it distracted her sister from drilling her any further.

"I don't know." Kimberly searched her mind for a plausible explanation and could think of only one. "A couple of the models I worked with last week did mention coming down with a bout of the flu over the past month. Maybe I caught something from one of them." The coffee maker buzzed, and Kimberly jumped up to turn it off. Halfway to the counter, she felt lightheaded, and her legs grew weak beneath her. She grabbed the edge of the sink, right before her legs gave out.

"Kimberly!" Carly scrambled out of her chair and rushed over to her sister. "We have to get you to the doctor. We can go to one of those twenty-four clinics. You might be dehydrated or, or, I don't know," Carly rambled while assisting Kimberly into a kitchen chair. "Stay right here while I get our coats."

Kimberly bobbed her head weakly. She did not have the strength to argue with Carly. Kim didn't dare tell her that this was the third time, in the last month, that she had nearly fainted. Her sister would surely panic from that news.

150

"Here, let me help you put this on." Carly, in typical fashion, Kimberly noted, took control of the situation. She had her own coat on and held Kimberly's open for her.

"Carly, I can put my own coat on. I'm not dying. I got dizzy, that's all. I probably have the flu, and it's left me a little weak." The 'month-long flu' she realized and hoped there was such a thing.

****

"Hello, Ms. Urbane. I'm Doctor Hayes," a middle-aged man with graying temples informed her soon after she was seated on top of the examining table.

"Let's see," the doctor murmured as he looked over her chart. "Seems as you fainted this afternoon—"

"Almost fainted."

"Ah, yes, almost fainted. You think it may be the flu. Why is that, Ms. Urbane? Have you been exposed to anyone with the flu?" he asked with a pleasant smile.

"Ah, well, I think so. I'm a photographer, and some people I worked with last week mentioned that they had the flu recently."

"That may very well be your problem then, Ms. Urbane, but just in case, I need to ask you some questions. First, how long have you been having flu symptoms?"

"Actually, a month, maybe a little longer. Maybe two?"

The doctor looked up from his note pad. His eyes squinted in concentration. "I see," he mumbled and jotted down some notes. "Perhaps you better explain your flu symptoms to me."

Kimberly squirmed on top of the examining table, her hands clasped tightly together. Doctors had made her nervous since childhood, and Dr. Hayes was no different. Despite his small gestures to make her comfortable, she still felt uneasy when she answered his questions. "Well, I've lost my appetite recently. Food sort of turns my stomach, I guess you could say," she told him and laughed uneasily. "I get dizzy occasionally and sometimes I feel warm, and the next minute I'm freezing." She shrugged, unable to think of any other symptoms.

"Hmm," Dr. Hayes said, as he wrote furiously on his notepad. "Anything else, Ms. Urbane? Shortness of breath? Loss of vision?" Kimberly shook her head. Loss of vision? What sort of flu virus strand was this?

"Ms. Urbane." He scribbled several words and then looked up from his notepad. "When was your last menstrual cycle?"

"My last menstrual cycle?" Kimberly mumbled and then realized she wasn't sure. "I, ah, well. I've never been regular. Sometimes I skip a month...I don't know for sure," she stammered. "Maybe two months ago? Or almost three? I'm not sure."

"I see," the doctor replied in a way that did not reduce her building anxiety. "I'd like to take a test first, but I think I may know what our problem is Ms. Urbane."

"You do? What is it?" For the first time, she was frightened that something may be seriously wrong with her. She pulled her lower lip between her teeth, her eyes large, and fearful.

"I think we better wait until I know for sure before we discuss it. Now, please relax while I call the nurse in. There's a simple test I'd like you to take."

****

Carly looked up from her magazine just as Kimberly walked out into the waiting room. Her sister's eyes widened at the sight of her, and Kimberly was tempted to laugh. Only tempted, because there was nothing funny about the doctor's diagnosis.

"Kimberly, what is it? What's wrong?" Carly questioned, fear evident in her tone. She hopped up from her seat and followed Kimberly out of the clinic's revolving door. She half-hoped Carly hadn't followed her, as she was in no mood to explain anything to her sister right now, not when she had yet to figure things out herself.

"Kimberly, you're scaring me. What is it?" Carly demanded from behind her.

Kimberly spun around and Carly's eyes widened when she looked up at her. Kimberly knew she should be reassuring her sister, rather than let her think the worse, but she wasn't thinking clearly, not yet.

"Oh no."

"Please take me home," Kimberly whispered in a tight voice. Sheer terror crossed her younger sister's perfect features, and Kimberly shook her head in frustration.

"What is it? What's wrong?"

"Carly, please just take me home. I'm not dying if that's what you're worried about. I'd rather not talk about it while we are standing in front of the clinic, however. We'll talk when we get home."

Carly took her car keys out of her purse and shook them at her sister. "Kimberly, I can't believe you sometimes. You walk out of the clinic looking worse than when you walked in. What do you want me to think?" She quickly followed on her sister's heels. "Do we need to stop at the pharmacy and pick up a prescription or anything else?"

"No, it's not necessary. Just take me home."

Kimberly sat down in the front seat of her sister's BMW,

buckled her seatbelt, and then closed her eyes for the duration of the ride home from the clinic.

****

"I'm not waiting another minute for you to tell me what's wrong," Carly demanded with a careless toss of her jacket over a kitchen chair. They had driven the fifteen-minute drive home in silence, which for Carly was probably a record, Kimberly thought, each of their nerves on edge for the entire trip.

Kimberly tossed her coat over her sister's and then walked over to the sink. She poured herself a glass of water and swiftly drained the contents. She placed her glass down on the counter and turned around to face her sister. She leaned against the back of the counter and lifted her hand to brush a wayward curl from her face. "Well, I don't have the flu." She looked directly at her sister and then laughed without a trace of humor.

Carly wrinkled her finely carved eyebrows in confusion. "Then, what's the problem?"

"The problem is not what I have. It's what I am."

"'What I am? Stop playing games, Kimberly, and tell me what's wrong."

"Okay. Here it goes, and brace yourself sis, because you're going to need it. I'm pregnant." Kimberly watched her sister's expression go from annoyance to stunned silence. Carly Urbane was finally shocked speechless. If the whole situation weren't so serious, Kim would be tempted to laugh. "And don't you dare ask, Carly, because it's Jake's. There's been no one else. I swear." It was the truth. There had been no one in the two years prior to Jake and no one in the nearly ten weeks since he'd left. As incredulous as it seemed, Jake was the father of the tiny baby growing inside of her.

154

"Oh, wow," Carly choked out from her spot on the kitchen chair. "Oh, double wow," she repeated, bringing her hand to cover her mouth. "Kimberly, how?"

Kimberly folded her arms in front of her and tilted her head in a way that told Carly she certainly wasn't going to explain that part. Kimberly blushed just thinking of the times she had made love with Jake. The incredible night they had spent together and then the fast and furiously passionate lovemaking the following morning flashed before her eyes, and she had to shake herself out of the memory.

"That's not what I mean, Kimberly. Jake told you about his, ah, problem, didn't he?"

"Yes." She sighed. "I don't know how either. I asked the doctor the same question."

"And—"

"And he says it has to do with chemistry or something like that. I don't know."

"What?"

"I told the doctor about Jake's case of the mumps, and he said that's more of a wife's tale than anything else. Sterility does happen in some very rare cases, but it's highly unlikely. As for Jake and his ex-wife's problems, the doctor explained that sometimes it's a matter of chemistry, combined with a whole lot of stress. He said he hears of cases all the time where people divorce because they can't have children. Then, they marry someone else, and within a couple of years they find themselves with a whole house full of children."

"I can't believe it," Carly stated incredulously. "Jake's going to be thrilled."

"No, he's not, Carly, because I'm not telling him."

"What?" Carly gasped. "Of course you're going to tell him. He's the baby's father. He has the right to know."

"He gave up his rights when he left me—"

155

"He didn't know. Give him the benefit of the doubt," Carly interrupted.

"No. You don't understand, Carly. You weren't there. You didn't have your heart shredded to pieces when Jake told me he didn't love me. He said he liked me, but he didn't love me. And...and that he no longer wanted the family thing."

Tears streamed down her cheeks, and Carly stared back at her as if she wasn't making any sense, which she wasn't.

"You mean Jake suspected you were pregnant before he left?"

"Of course not." Kimberly exhaled an exaggerated breath. "He spoke in general terms. Carly, I begged him to stay. Literally begged him. Do you know how humiliating that is? Especially when he throws it back in your face with something as unemotional and detached as 'we can always be friends'? No. No way, Carly. I am not contacting him. I know he would sacrifice his happiness for the sake of the baby, and we would both be miserable that way."

"And how do you plan to keep Jake from finding out?"

"I thought about that on the way home from the clinic. First of all, Jake is out of the country, so there won't be a chance of us running into each other. Secondly, Jake would never suspect the child was his because he thinks he can't have children." And, she added to herself, I can't tell him, because I'm terrified of his rejection. Once was enough for one lifetime.

"Don't you think people are going to question who the father of your baby is? Not many people know that Jake can't have children, Kimberly. Or thought he couldn't, I guess is more accurate now." She twisted her hands together in her lap as she looked over at her sister.

"Not many people knew he lived here. I doubt Jake will ever be a consideration among the gossip mongers," she responded more harshly than she intended. She had enough problems at the moment without having to worry about a bunch of busybodies. Even though she could hardly consider her parents as busybodies, there was no doubt that they would question her repeatedly about the father of her baby when they returned from their year living abroad with her Dad's sister in Ireland. Ask? she mentally repeated. No, her parents would not respect her privacy enough to simply ask her. It was more likely that they would demand.

"Kimberly, what are you going to do?"

"I don't know yet." She stared back at her sister and told her, "and you are not to breathe a word to anyone, do you hear me Carly? No one. Thank God Mom and Dad are in Ireland right now staying with Aunt May. At least I won't have to deal with them for another two or three months," Kimberly muttered. How she would avoid her brother George was another thing. She cringed at the thought of her overprotective brother learning that his unmarried sister was pregnant and by one of his closest friends. She was grateful Carly hadn't thought of George's reaction either, or they would spend the afternoon in debate over it.

Carly glanced at her watch. "Look, Kimberly, I've got to go and get the girls. Why don't you lay down for a while and take it easy? I'll call you later tonight."

"Sure." Kimberly followed Carly to the front of the house and hugged her tightly before she left. After closing the door, Kimberly turned around and pressed her back against the door frame. "What am I going to do?" She repeated the question over and over on her way up the stairs to her bedroom.

Exhausted, both mentally and physically, she flounced down on top of her bed. She stared up at the ceiling, her eyes open but not seeing anything in particular. She sighed longingly and placed her hand on her still flat stomach. What was she going to do? That was a very good question. She could always move and leave California. That way she would be able to avoid questions about the baby's father. She gave the idea only a few moments of thought. That would be running away from my problems, not solving them. Besides, she didn't want to give up her house or move from her family. No, moving was definitely out of the question.

Her job, she groaned inwardly. How would she travel with a small baby in tow? Could she really leave her child every day, sometimes for twelve hours at a time? She couldn't. Although only aware of the life that grew inside of her for less than an hour, her maternal instincts had already kicked in at full blast. She would need to alter her work schedule somehow. After some consideration, the idea of a portrait studio began to take hold of her mind. Somewhere in town possibly, where clients could come to her. Kimberly made a mental note to investigate the idea first thing tomorrow morning.

Now to tackle her biggest problem: what would she tell people? She could always say she had gone to a sperm bank, she reasoned. The concept was very trendy. Kimberly shuddered. The idea of carrying a stranger's child inside of her did not appeal to her, even if it wasn't true. A one-night stand while in Paris might be a good excuse, she mused, and then killed the idea. Visions of her parents' look of horror flashed before her eyes. They would be mortified at such behavior from their daughter. Despite the fact that she was thirty-one years old and living on her own, her parents maintained old-fashioned ideals, ones that did not include their daughter sleeping with strangers.

Maybe she would just tell people the truth. She had fallen in love with someone, and unfortunately, he didn't return her love. They no longer saw each other, having gone their separate ways. It wasn't a lie; that's for sure. Kimberly reached for a pillow and clenched it tightly to her. Why, Jake? Why didn't you love me? We could have been so happy together. Kimberly yawned. The day's events had taken a toll on her weary body. She curled tightly into a ball, and a faint sob slipped from her lips before she drifted off to sleep.

Chapter 14

"On behalf of the crew of flight 506, headed to Lima, Peru, we welcome you aboard. For those of you who have been with us since Miami, we thank you once again for flying with us today and hope you have enjoyed traveling with us. We are waiting for approval for take-off, and we apologize for the delay. If there is anything we can do to make you more comfortable until we receive approval for take-off, please don't hesitate to contact one of the flight attendants on-board. Weather reports for Lima, Peru indicate that today's high is sixty-seven degrees, cooling off later this evening. Our flight time from Caracas to Lima is estimated at four hours and five minutes."

Jake shifted in his seat, glad at least for the comforts of first class on what was actually a short flight for him compared to his typical overseas flights. He normally brought a book with him to pass the time, preferably a mystery, but he had forgotten to grab one from the airport newsstand. The last six months in Saudi Arabia had provided him with little time for leisure activity, and the latest best seller had been the last thing on his mind. Now, with no more than a plane ride as a reprieve, he was headed to Peru. The revolutionaries, known to the world as the "Shining Path" terrorist group, had taken responsibility for several bombings in the last week, and tensions had risen among the civilians. It was rumored that all hell was about to break loose, and he would be right in the middle of it. And why not? What else did he have to go home to? Springtime in San Francisco? Budding flowers and romances? Not hardly.

"Well, mercy. I wonder how long this delay is going to be. Young man, would you mind reaching up and handing me my bag? It's in the compartment above your head."

"Ah, sure." Jake glanced at the woman seated next to him. Her hair was pulled on top of her head in a silver crown, in much the same as grandmothers styled it on old television dramas, he thought with a hint of humor. Her plump face sat on top of an even plumper body. She wore a dress adorned with large pink and purple flowers, once again, just like they did on television, and he laughed to himself.

"It's the paisley bag, dear."

"Why thank you so much, young man," she bubbled when he placed the oversized bag on her ample lap.

"Ah, here is the one I want." She sighed in relief and pulled a large photo album out of the bag. "Would you mind, dear?" She handed the bag back to him with a pat on hand.

"No problem." Jake's amusement with the old woman grew exponentially.

"I take my photo albums with me everywhere I go. Why, I would be lost without them. Look, here's a picture of my dear Howard, bless his soul." She fluttered over a black-and-white photograph.

Jake obliged the old woman by looking at the picture of her husband, obviously taken decades ago. Jake smiled warmly at her and then motioned to the flight attendant for a magazine. He didn't want to be rude, but perhaps if the woman thought he was immersed in an article, she would refrain from showing him every picture in her cumbersome album. Somehow, he didn't think it would work, but at least it was worth a try. There has to be a hundred pages in that thing, he estimated. He turned once again to try to capture the flight attendant's attention.

"Yes Mr. Taylor?"

"I'd like a magazine, preferably Newsweek or Time, if you have it."

"Certainly, Mr. Taylor." Jake settled back into his seat. He closed his eyes, although he was anything but tired, and nearly jumped out of his seat in reaction to his companion's high-pitched voice.

"Heavens, here is our wedding picture. Can you believe that's me? I wasn't much of a looker back in nineteen-sixty-four either, but my dear Howard didn't care. He loved me just the way I am, and thank God for that, or else I may not have ten beautiful children to share my life with now. Not to mention my twenty-seven adorable grandchildren," she added with a glowing look of adoration at several of the photographs.

"Ten children?" Jake repeated to himself with a shudder that ran along his spine. No wonder the woman will chat with a complete stranger; she's out of her mind. Ten children, really? His interest was piqued. Unable to prevent his curiosity from demanding to be satisfied, he asked, "You had ten kids?"

"There's Howard holding our Betsy. What's that dear?" she crooned happily before she looked up from her album.

"I just said, ah, you had ten children?"

"Hmm, I guess that depends how you look at it, dear. I'm being cryptic, aren't I? Annoys Emily to death-- she's my eighth--when I leave her hanging like I do." The old woman laughed; her pale blue eyes sparkled with merriment. She patted Jake's hand reassuringly and settled deeper into her seat.

Now, I've done it, Jake thought hopelessly. The eccentric old woman would talk his ear off for the entire journey, and he had provoked it. He returned her smile with one of his own, as he waited for her to elaborate.

"I say depends, dear, because it really does. You see, as a young girl I was in a very unfortunate accident. Took me months before I could walk again. After a year of rehabilitation, I looked as good as new on the outside. Unfortunately, my insides didn't fare as well. I met my loving Howard at that time. I had just turned twenty." She leaned her large girth close to Jake, and in a conspiratorial voice, whispered into his ear, "I was messed up in my, hmm, lady parts. Not that I couldn't be a wife to my sweet Howard, I assure you, but I couldn't have children."

She returned to her former position of shaking her head and clucked her tongue several times on the roof of her mouth. "Well, I was just beside myself, I tell you. Not being a real beauty myself, I questioned what I really had to offer Howard. Let me tell you young man, my Howard was quite a catch in those days. He was being groomed to take over his father's grocery store, not to mention that he was quite a looker." She clucked her tongue again, emphasizing her good fortune so long ago.

"Now let me tell you, I was up front with Howard from the beginning. I wasn't one of those girls who played games, not me, not Henrietta Zarlong. Anyway, my dear Howard, do you know what he said to me? He said, 'Henny, I love you for yourself. If that means it's just the two of us, then that makes me a greedy man, and I don't care, because I'd love nothing more to spend my life with just you.'" She dabbed at the corners of her eyes with her handkerchief and then proceeded to blow her nose into it.

"My, I did love that crazy old coot so much." She laughed into her hanky.

"You were able to have children after all. That's great." Jake smiled back at her.

"Heavens no," she chirped with a wave of her hand in the air. "We adopted them, all ten of them. We agreed to just one at first, but by our third wedding anniversary there were four little mouths sitting around the dinner table with us. Times were tough back then, you know? There were so many needy children roaming the streets. By the time we celebrated our fifteenth wedding anniversary, we were raising ten children."

Jake swallowed. Adoption? Howard and Henrietta had adopted ten children? He decided he could be on a first name basis with them now that he practically knew their whole life story. Had they been happy? She sure made it seem so. "Did you, ah, ever regret it?" Jake realized his question held far more importance to him than idle curiosity.

Henrietta leaned over and patted him on the arm. "My goodness, no, dear. Never. I loved each one of those children from the time I first held them in my arms. They were my babies from the moment I laid my eyes on them."

He held a glass of bourbon he had ordered when he first boarded the plane. He felt his hand shake, and the glass rattled against the tray table. Adoption? He repeated the word over and over in his head. Brenda had scorned the idea, but Kimberly? God, yes. Loving, caring, Kimberly, would have jumped at the idea. What had he done? How could he have not thought of this during all the sleepless nights he spent wishing she was in his arms? And was it too late? Six months was a long time to be able to forget someone. Perhaps Kimberly had already done just that.

"Why, I'm on my way to Peru to visit my daughter Caroline now. Her husband is a diplomat and has been stationed in Lima for some time now. She's invited me to stay permanently, but I couldn't do that to my youngest one, Ann, why—"

Henrietta's voice droned on and on, but Jake was no longer listening. Instead, he heard other voices that echoed through his head.

"I love you, Jake."

"Kim, I don't love you."

"I've loved you forever."

"I don't want an 'us' with anyone."

"I only need you, Jake."

"I don't want the family thing anymore."

"I would do anything for you, Jake."

"Take care of yourself."

"Goodbye."

My God, I've been such a fool! "Excuse me, Miss, excuse me?"

"We're still looking for those magazines, Mr. Taylor. Can I get you something else in the meantime?"

"No, you don't understand." He undid his seat belt and stood up. "I have to get off this plane." His eyes darted toward the exit door and then to the overhead compartment where he stowed his duffle bag.

"I'm sorry, Mr. Taylor, but that's not possible. We just pushed away from the jet bridge. You'll have to return to your seat," she instructed with a perfunctory smile.

"There has to be a way. I have to get off this plane!" And on to another one going to San Francisco. Going to Kimberly.

"I'm sorry Mr. Taylor, but if you'll look out the window, we are approaching the runway. You need to sit down."

"I, I didn't notice." Jake returned to his seat. He buckled his seat belt over his waist and shook his head in defeat. He would be in Lima in less than five hours. He would just have to wait it out. He would call Kimberly when they landed, and hopefully, if she agreed, she would be waiting for him at the San Francisco airport in another twenty-four hours. Only one more lonely night spent fighting off the erotic images of Kimberly wrapped tightly in his embrace until he actually held her again. What was one more night, he conceded, when he once believed he had been sentenced to an eternity without her?

Jake sighed deeply, temporarily resigned to his fate. He turned to Henrietta and offered her an apologetic smile for his previous interruption of her story. "Excuse me, Henrietta, may I call you Henrietta? Would you like to show me the rest of your photo album?"

The elderly woman beamed with pleasure and delightedly informed Jake that she had three more photo albums in her bag. Certainly, enough pictures, she assured him, to keep them entertained for the entire flight.

****

Jake threw his knapsack over his shoulder. His eyes darted around the small, congested airport for a charging station. He swore swiftly under his breath once he recalled that South American countries didn't offer many of the amenities he took for granted in the United States. He couldn't believe that he had forgotten to charge his cell, and now it was dead. As he looked across the terminal for a wall outlet, he saw Henrietta's family circle around the elderly woman. Each member took turns showering her with hugs. He smiled at the tender sight. If the old woman only knew how much she had helped him realize that he and Kimberly had a real chance at love, she'd probably add their photos to her album. "Jake! Jake! Over here," a deep male voice called over numerous heads.

Jake turned to see several cameramen and another journalist he had worked with the last time he was in Peru. He picked up his carry-on bag and walked over to the men. He had learned to travel light a long time ago. His luggage consisted of a carry-on bag and a small knapsack. "Well, this is some welcome. I certainly didn't expect this big of a reception." Normally, he met up with the rest of the crew at their hotel after he had checked in and secured his luggage in his room.

"Jake, we've been waiting for you since four o'clock. Your plane was due in over two hours ago," said Tom, a small, wiry man with a dark beard and a large video camera propped up at his side.

"We had to avoid some severe weather, which took us out of our way," Jake responded to the cameraman. "What gives, anyway? Why are you guys here?" He was anxious to call Kimberly and, with any luck, be on the next plane back to San Francisco.

"Three Catholic priests were found slain this afternoon outside of Lima. The whole country is in chaos. The Shining Path is refusing to claim responsibility and, instead, is blaming the government, and the government is blaming the Shining Path. People are filling the streets in protest. It's a mess out there. Jake, we've got to get out of Lima and to where the priests were found before nightfall. The President is planning to place a curfew on the city. The military is everywhere. We won't be able to get near the site until daybreak if that happens," explained Luke, a thickly built, scruffy man and one of the Associated Press's leading journalists.

"Damn." He looked at each of the men. "Where's Stevens?" he asked, referring to the other news journalist his network had sent to Peru months ago to cover the story while Jake was on a leave of absence.

"Stevens is down with some bug, caught it while we followed some guerillas rumored to have defected from the Shining Path. Conditions were pretty rough near the river. We think he may have caught something from a bug bite."

"Most likely from one of the local female bugs," Tom muttered, and his companions each responded with a chuckle under their breaths.

Luke gave Tom a silencing look and then returned his attention to Jake. "Jake, we've got the Jeep parked right outside the front doors. We've got to get out of here now—"

"I can't. I've got to charge my phone because I need to make—"

"Jake, we need you to go live today in front of the cameras. We're running out of time."

"What about you, Luke? Can't you do the story?" Jake questioned the other journalist before he glanced at his watch.

"No way, Jake. You know I'm a print guy only. I'm no good in front of the camera. You have to do this. We've got nobody else with Stevens out of commission."

Jake ran his hand over his face, and he brushed against the dense edges of stubble growing on his unshaven jawbone. He needed to get back on a plane to San Francisco, but his sense of duty nagged at him. He had worked damn hard as a journalist. He knew what a story like this would mean if they could get it on the air. He had spent over two years in South America before going to the Middle East, fighting to bring to the attention of the American public the thousands of innocent people who suffered because of the wars between the rebel guerillas and the government.

He wanted to walk away from the problems of South America and go home, home to Kimberly, to begin a life together. But he couldn't. Not yet. He would wait until Stevens was back on his feet, and then Jake would be on the next plane back to California. "Okay, let's go." He held up his hand. "But I need to make a call first," he told them, and each of the four other men stopped in their tracks. "Can I borrow someone's cell?"

"Take mine." Tom reached into his vest pocket for his cell. He pulled it out and handed it over to Jake.

Jake gratefully took the cell from him, eager to call Kimberly. "Why don't I meet you guys out in the Jeep... I'll only be a minute." He looked expectantly at each of them. The group grumbled, but agreed to meet him outside.

"Think he's calling a woman?" Jake heard one of them ask as they walked away. He was pretty sure Luke was the one to reply. "No way, he's a journalist, remember? What woman would want a man who loves the thrill of a breaking story more than a soft body curled up beside him?"

"None that we know," the deep voice of one the cameramen joked and sent the rest of the group into a roar of laughter.

Jake punched the first few digits of Kimberly's phone number into the cell and paused. Luke, Tom, all of them, were wrong. He had changed. From now on, he listened to his heart, instead of his head. Kimberly came first in his life, starting... starting as soon as Stevens was well enough to take over again. Damn, he wasn't off to a great start, but he would get there. He knew he would. Jake entered the last of Kimberly's cell number into the phone with a renewed sense of determination. His heart beat rapidly in his chest when he heard the line connect, and Kimberly's phone rang on the other end. The connection was marginal at best, the static vibrated in his ear.

"Hi—"

"Kimberly, it's Jake."

"...I'm not able to come to the phone right now; Please leave a message at the tone with your name and number, and I will try to get back to you." *BEEP*.

Damn, voicemail. He hated leaving messages on voicemail. He never knew what to say and always ended up tongue-tied because of it. "Ah, yeah, hi Kimberly. This is Jake. I've just arrived in Lima, Peru. My plane was delayed because of some severe weather in the area," God, he made no sense. "Anyway, I guess you're busy. I'll try you tomorrow. Take care." He pushed the end button on the cellphone and temporarily placed it in his jacket pocket. "My plane was delayed because of some severe weather in the area?" he repeated out loud. "Of all the stupid things to say." He berated himself over and over again as he exited the airport. By the time he reached the Jeep, he was in a rotten mood and eager to get his report over so he could get out of Peru.

****

Jake unlocked the door of his hotel room with a tired sigh. He threw his bag on a nearby chair and sat down on the bed. He was exhausted, bone-tired. For three long days and three longer nights, he and his team had interviewed everyone from a Catholic nun to a homeless teen about the recent killings of the priests outside of Lima. Despite the poverty and political unrest, the Peruvians maintained a rigid faith in God. The majority of them were Roman Catholics. The death of the three priests weighed heavily on their souls and minds. People were scared. The President tried his best to maintain peace among his people, but Jake was afraid it wasn't enough. All hell was about to break loose in Peru. He could feel it in his blood.

Now back at the hotel, the reporters and camera crew had only to complete the wrap-up of their last segment, and they then could call it a night. Jake decided he would call Kimberly and then rejoin his team to film the final wrap-up, so he could return to his room to take a shower and then sleep for a good eight hours. He reached over to the nightstand and grabbed the phone from its resting place. Despite his best efforts to make it happen, his cell would no longer charge. He planned to replace his cell when he was back in the States, but for now, the hotel phone would have to do. He picked up the receiver, requested an outside line from the hotel operator, and then dialed her number. Hopefully, this time, she would answer.

Once again, as in the airport, the sound of the call rang in his ear, and it caused his heart pound in his chest. For the past six months, he hadn't allowed himself to think about how much he missed her, how much he needed to be with her. While in Saudi Arabia, he had never once allowed himself any fantasies about Kimberly, at least not consciously. The nights were a different story. But now, now his hope was renewed.

Jake bristled as he listened to the call go directly into voicemail. Again, a recording repeated, "I'm not able to come to the phone right now, please—" He disconnected the call without leaving a message.

For the third time today, his call went directly into voicemail. Was there something wrong with her cell? Had she forgotten to charge it as she had at least a dozen times in the weeks he had spent with her?

Damn, he needed to talk to her. Her family must keep in contact with her, he decided determinedly. They would know whether there was something wrong with her phone, or not, or could at least get a message to her that he needed to speak to her and to plug in her phone. The only problem was that he didn't know any of the Urbane's phone numbers by memory. The only numbers he had memorized were his editor's, Kimberly's, and

Zane's. Why not? He reached over and picked up the phone receiver.

Zane answered on the third ring. "Speak to me."

"How about trying hello once in a while, Zane? Maybe people wouldn't hang up on you so often."

"Very funny, Jake," came his reply, and then he laughed into the receiver. "You know women never hang up on me, and who cares about the men."

Jake chuckled in response. His brother may be laughing, but he spoke the truth. Zane Taylor attracted women like bees to honey. Jake wouldn't be surprised if Zane entertained some leggy blonde right now, which reminded him to get to the point of his conversation before his brother hung up on him. "Zane, I need a favor. I need you to reach out to Carly and ask her to contact Kimberly. I've tried Kimberly several times, and her cell keeps going directly into voicemail."

"You want to speak to Kimberly? What for?" Zane asked, not bothering to disguise his surprise. Jake had provided him with a minimal amount of details when Jake had returned home to deal with the passing of their grandfather. Whether Zane had been shocked to hear that Jake had been staying with Kimberly for several weeks, Zane didn't say. He wasn't much on relationships and typically avoided providing advice on the subject. As a result, Jake hadn't bothered sharing the details with him, good or bad.

"The sweet Peruvian senoritas not treating you well? They do have some beautiful women there, don't they Jake? Did I ever tell you about the time I was in Brazil during a break in my residency, and I got caught in a rain storm with this woman, Marcella, I think her name was. Anyway, you want to talk about—"

"Zane!" He had no doubt that Zane had a story that involved him and some woman in every country in the world. There wasn't a continent the younger Taylor

172

had left unscathed. He was a notorious playboy with the looks and charisma that allowed him to be just that. Normally, Jake would listen if only with half of an ear, but now was not one of those times.

"Zane, I did not call you from Peru to discuss your worldwide conquests. I need you to contact Carly."

"I can't believe it. Down by one, and he misses the free throw!" Zane shouted in the background. "Sorry about that, Jake. The Warriors are playing Chicago tonight. Anyway, why would Carly get a message to Kimberly for me, or worse, for you? In case you never noticed, the Urbane girls and I never really ran in the same circles. Far too studious for my tastes. Not that studious is bad, especially when they're women who are six-feet tall with legs that never end, like this lady anthropologist I met in Egypt. Now there was a woman who didn't know the meaning of—"

"Zane. For God's sake." Jake groaned into the phone. "Look, can you please call Carly and have her get a message to Kimberly? I'd call myself, but my cell's dead, and I have to be downstairs to meet my team for the wrap-up of our last segment. Please tell her I will call her in approximately 3 hours and to have her phone charged." Although the more he thought about it, the more he believed his calls were intentionally being sent to voicemail. He had left a message on her voicemail three days ago, and now every time he called, it didn't even ring, it just went directly to voicemail. There didn't seem to be any other reason, except that Kimberly didn't want to speak to him.

"Aw, Jake. It's the fourth quarter with four minutes to go. I have big money going on this game. If the Warriors win, they're going to the playoffs. Why don't you call Carly yourself?"

"Zane, I already explained. Why is it that you have time to tell me about your numerous sexual exploits in every God forsaken country in the world, but you don't have time to make a phone call for me?"

"Jesus, Jake. Don't get all bent out of shape. I'll call her. Give me your hotel number, and I'll call you back in ten minutes," Zane shot back.

"Fine." He gave Zane the number and added, "call me back." The dial tone hummed in Jake's ear before he had the chance to say goodbye.

Jake walked into the bathroom and turned on the light. He was in desperate need of a shower... three days of dirt and grime lay on top of his skin. He could be in and out before Zane called back. Several minutes passed while he stood under the showerhead. The lukewarm water was running over his weary body when he remembered another shower over six months ago. All too quickly, images of Kimberly rubbing soapy hands over his naked chest was more than he could handle. He turned the water to cool. When that didn't work, he turned the water off and stepped out of the shower.

He glanced at his watch lying on top of the bathroom sink. Another five minutes passed, and Zane had yet to call him back.

"She forwarded her phone to voicemail. I know she did." He reached into his duffle bag and pulled out a fresh pair of jeans. "Or maybe it was just a coincidence. Maybe her cell broke. Mine has, so it was entirely possible that she could also—" Jake stopped himself short.

He stood in front of the mirror, the comb he held in his hand suspended in mid-air. He stared at his reflection. He looked older. The lines that crept out from the corners of his eyes were deeper than he remembered them. He was thinner too. His cheek bones protruded to sharp angles from underneath his tanned skin. The last six months had taken a toll on him. He admitted it. Regardless of how much he had tried, Kimberly was the dream at night he never could quite sleep through, the gnawing emptiness in his stomach no amount of food could ever assuage. He needed her like he had never needed anything, or anyone, in his life. For the last six months, he had been merely existing, never really living.

He stared into the mirror with a renewed sense of being. He was ready to live, ready to fulfill his dreams, and ready to get rid of the pain eating at his gut. He sat down on the edge of his bed and reached for his wallet. He pulled out a battered picture he kept buried deep behind his credit card and driver's license. The photograph's edges were frayed and bent due to his daily need to reassure himself it was still there, tucked away for safe keeping. His lips curved in a bittersweet smile. He held on tightly to the picture of Kimberly and Daisy, posed graciously for him on the front steps of her house.

He sighed. By ignoring his calls, perhaps Kimberly was showing him how deeply affected she was by his absence. Maybe she felt the same aching loneliness during the night that he did, the need to feel him next to her overwhelming her as it did him.

Maybe, and most likely, she was so mad at him that she refused to speak to him. Or, he didn't want to think about it. It might be that she wasn't affected at all.

Six months, almost seven, was a long time, long enough to move on with your life. He visibly shuddered at the thought of Kimberly involved with another man.

Rattled by the idea of Kimberly moving on without him, he walked over to the hotel telephone, no longer willing to wait for Zane to return his call. He dialed his brother's phone number and simultaneously took a deep, calming breath. A million thoughts ran through his head. What if Kimberly was involved with someone else? What if she had told her boyfriend about his call, and the boyfriend had then demanded that she not speak to Jake?

"Zane?"

"Jake! You nearly gave me a heart attack. Could you try not to shout in my ear next time?"

"Sorry," Jake mumbled. "Did you find out anything?"

"I spoke to Carly," Zane answered evasively.

"And—"

"And she says Kimberly doesn't want to speak to you. Carly wouldn't forward her a message from you, either."

"Damn."

"Jake," Zane stated slyly. "What exactly happened between you and Kimberly? I know the two of you lived under the same roof for several weeks. Two single, healthy adults, things are bound to happen. But what went wrong? And why is it that six months after you've moved out of her place that you're suddenly so hot to get in touch with her?"

"Zane, let's just say I don't have your finesse when it comes to relationships." *Not even close.* "Anyway, you have more important things to worry about right now."

"I do?"

"You do. Starting with the purchase of some furniture and a good mattress set for the spare bedroom in that bachelor pad of yours. Because, little brother, I'm taking the next flight out of this South American jungle and coming home." He didn't plan on staying with his brother for long, but he definitely felt less confident that Kimberly would take him back with open arms than he did an hour ago, and it worried him that it might be an extended stay if he couldn't convince her to forgive him.

Zane whistled into the phone. "Who would have thought my big brother would race home to play 'me Tarzan, you Jane' with an unsuspecting female? I didn't think you had it in you."

"I don't know that I do, Zane. But I do know it's something I should have done a long time ago," he said more to himself than to his brother. "I'll see you sometime tomorrow night." Jake stared at the telephone for several minutes after he placed it on its receiver.

It was time to go home.

Home.

To Kimberly. Only twenty-four more hours. He visibly shuddered. For the first time in months, Jake felt some relief from the heaviness in his heart.

Chapter 15

Jake parked the four-door sedan next to the street curb and didn't bother to lock it. There had been a waiting list at the airport car rental for anything sportier than the standard rentals, and he was not prepared to wait. There would be time later to trade the car in for something comparable to the Ferrari he had rented the last time he had been in town. His steps faltered. He was in town to stay this time. He could actually join the rest of society and purchase a car rather than survive on rentals.

He crossed the street and stopped to look at the stucco bungalow before he continued down the sidewalk. Little had changed during the six and half months he had been gone. The white wicker furniture still adorned the front porch, and pots filled with flowering red and purple bougainvillea hung from the porch ceiling. He hoped this was an indication that he'd find everything else the same.

He brushed the palms of his hands against the soft denim of his jeans. He climbed the wooden porch steps and stood in front of the screen door. He pressed the doorbell, and the musical chimes that Kimberly loved so much echoed through the house. He nearly crushed the bouquet of roses he clutched tightly in his hand. What if she's moved on? Without him?

"Come on in, Susan. I'll be right down," a voice called from deep within the house. He tensed, a stream of sensations cursed through his body to settle at the core of his heart.

Jake accepted her invitation, although not intended for him, and opened the screen door. He stepped into the foyer and hesitated. He expected Daisy to charge at him at any moment, and he hoped the giant fur ball would remember him. No sign of Daisy anywhere. She was probably in the backyard, lounged in the warm spring sun. Some watch dog Kimberly had herself. The corners of his generous mouth curled upward in half of a grin.

He turned his head to the sound of deliberate footsteps steadily descending the stairwell.

"Sorry to keep you waiting, Susan. I gathered the last of these clothes for the bazaar so you could take them—" Kimberly's labored breath was interrupted by her abrupt gasp.

"Jake!" She leaned back against the wall. "What are you doing here?" She glanced sharply at him and then back at the large basket of clothing she held in her arms. She was clearly surprised and something else. Frightened? But why?

"I thought you were, ah, my friend Susan... coming to collect some clothing for the church bazaar this weekend," she stammered in a shaky voice. She remained on the bottom step and leaned heavily against the wall for support.

Jake's bold gaze quickly skipped over the mound of clothing she carried and traveled upward to her face. She was lovely. Even with her wild mane of black curls piled high on her head and her face devoid of any make-up, he could think of her as nothing but breathtaking. Flawless. The memories he held of her over the last six and a half months had not done her justice. It was physically painful for him to think that he had actually walked away from her and from the love she had professed that she would always have for him.

"Can I take that basket for you? It looks like a pretty heavy load you have there."

"No. I mean, no thank you," she amended. "Susan should be here any minute to pick them up."

He narrowed his eyes but accepted her response. "I expected to be trampled by Daisy when I walked in. Is she out back?"

"Yes, she is. It's such a nice day..." Kimberly's voice trailed off.

She was obviously taken back by his unexpected visit, and he couldn't blame her. He was a bit overwhelmed himself. Her attempt at small talk was as feeble as his own. His eyes, hungry for the sight of her, settled on her face again. She was tense. Her chocolate eyes were large and alert.

To his puzzlement, she refused to put down the enormous basket of clothing she clutched like a lifeline. He watched her shift her weight to rest on her opposite foot, the movement awkward and seemingly painful for her.

"Kimberly, it really looks like you have quite a load in your hands. I'll tell you what, I'll trade you these flowers for your basket. That way you can find a vase for the poor wilting bunch, and I'll find an equally suitable home for your clothes until your friend shows up." Jake swiftly breached the distance between them and stood in front of her in less than two strides.

He reached out and grabbed the bulging basket from her grasp. She reacted by letting out a loud yelp of protest. "Jake, don't. I told you. I don't need—"

Kimberly's voice faded into the background. Jake stood dumbstruck before he took a hesitant step backwards. The basket of neatly folded clothing lay in a large puddle at their feet. The flowers lay strewn on top of them.

Time stopped. The only sound he was conscious of was the erratic beat of his heart pounding in his ears. He wasn't even aware that he had let go of the roses, until he spied them laying on top of the clothing. His gaze darted to the swelling girth of Kimberly's midriff. She was well into her pregnancy. Her stomach strained against the thin cotton of her maternity shirt.

"I, I'm sorry. I didn't know." His voice cracked, and the sound echoed through the quiet house. His breath was ragged. Time became temporarily suspended.

He finally dragged his eyes back to her face. This wasn't how he wanted to remember her, yet it would likely be the last time he ever saw her again, because there was no way he could remain in San Francisco now. The pink coloring that naturally stained her cheeks was gone. Her skin had paled to a ghostly white. Her dark chestnut eyes were wide, and tears glazed each of them. Her mouth molded into a small 'o' and her pouty lips weakly colored into the softest of pinks.

He closed his eyes and willed the sight before him to be only an illusion and the hurt that clenched at his soul to be only a figment of his imagination. He opened his eyes with a sense of dread, stared briefly at her stomach and then sagged his shoulders in defeat. "I won't bother you again."

He turned away from her, his feet weighed down with the anchor of despair as he walked away. His hand shook when he reached for the screen door and pulled it open far harder than necessary. He walked out onto the porch and extinguished a loud, pained sigh. The screen door slammed behind him.

He took the steps two at a time and stopped when he reached the edge of the sidewalk. A sharp pain clawed at his heart, and he felt light-headed. He walked away without taking a final glance behind him.

"Jake," he heard her call from the house. He increased the pace of his steps and crossed the street.

"Please Jake."

He heard the creak of the porch door but refused to turn around. He pulled his keys from his pocket as he approached the car. He kept his head lowered.

"Wait," she called to his retreating back.

"Jake, I have to talk to you. Please, you don't understand—"

The sound of screeching tires against asphalt assaulted the otherwise quiet morning. A loud thud followed and then silence. Jake stopped in mid-stride, paralyzed. "Please, God, no." He whipped around to look behind him.

"Kimberly—" He rushed to where she lay motionless in the middle of the suburban street.

The driver of the car approached him in near hysterics. "Oh man. I didn't see her... she ran out of nowhere, mister. Oh man, oh man," the teenage boy rushed on in a panic-filled voice.

Jake knelt down next to Kimberly's unmoving form. He wiped away the wild tangles of hair from her face. "Come on, sweetheart. Open your eyes," he urged in a shattered breath.

A small crowd gathered around them. Many ran from inside their homes at the sound of the commotion coming from the street. Jake sensed, rather than saw them, gather around. His head darted up. "Somebody, call an ambulance," he commanded in an unsteady voice. "Somebody, please call an ambulance!"

Chapter 16

Jake paced the noisy emergency waiting room with tense, anxious strides. He was oblivious to the numerous people being shuffled in and out of the area, many on stretchers or in wheelchairs. He focused on the door to the examining room, the same door the paramedics had carried Kimberly through over an hour ago. He should have told the hospital personnel to call the father of the baby when they had asked him for his name and Kimberly's, but he hadn't been thinking clearly, and he wasn't sure if he ever would again.

If anything happened to her... no, he wouldn't allow his thoughts to take that dark and narrow path. He had never considered himself a religious man, but now he found himself praying for God's assistance with each ticking of the clock on the emergency room wall.

"Jake. Jake," cried a voice from behind him.

"Carly." He practically crushed her in his embrace. He took in her tear stained cheeks, her normally immaculate facade shaken and disheveled, and he felt like crying himself, but seeing Carly release enough tears for both of them helped him to remain strong.

"Have you heard anything?" She pulled herself from his embrace to take a tissue from her purse.

"Not yet." He motioned to a pair of empty seats, as he realized his own need to sit down. He had been pacing the waiting room for over an hour. He could do with a strong cup of coffee, but that would have to wait until later. There wasn't a chance he was going to miss the doctor coming out of the door with news of Kimberly. He would sit here for days, if that was what it took.

"Jake what happened? I was at the movies with the girls and didn't get your message until twenty minutes ago. I was so upset. I don't think I understood any more than Kimberly and the name of the hospital."

"I'm sorry about that. I was rather upset myself. Carly... it's my fault that she was hit by a car. She called after to me to stop, and I didn't listen. I just kept walking away from her."

Confusion marred Carly's tear stained face. "Jake, whatever are you talking about? I didn't even know you were back in town, let alone you and Kimberly—"

"I flew in this morning from Peru. I met this woman on a plane from Venezuela... a grandmother of twenty-seven children." He caught the puzzled arch of Carly's perfectly formed brow, and he paused. He was rambling, something he never did. He was definitely on the verge of losing it. He shook his head, as he tried to make sense of the last few days.

"Anyway, she made me see the light, as the saying goes. She and her husband couldn't have children of their own, so they adopted. I got to thinking that maybe adoption could solve the problem, my problem, with Kimberly. The next thing I knew, I was on a plane back to San Francisco, even though I knew she didn't want to see me again." He exhaled a deep breath.

"And you came home to discover Kimberly pregnant. Very pregnant," Carly interjected with a nod of understanding.

"It was stupid, I know. I didn't even send her a text for over six months, and for some idiotic reason, I thought she would be waiting for me with open arms. I'm a fool." Jake leaned over and rested his elbows on his knees. He braced his face with his hands and shook his head in tired defeat.

"I didn't even realize she was pregnant when I first saw her. She had a large basket of clothes in her arms, for some damn bazaar or something. It looked heavy. I tried to take the basket from her. That's when I saw...I found out she was pregnant. I practically stormed out of the place. She followed me and called after me, but I wouldn't listen. I just needed to get out of there. She ran out into the street trying to reach me before I drove away, I guess. The car that hit her couldn't have been going that fast. I never even heard it approaching us. If anything happens to her, Carly—." Jake's voice cracked. He buried his face deeper into his hands.

Carly reached over and tenderly placed a hand on his back. "Jake, it's going to be all right. Kimberly needs us to be strong for her."

Jake shook his head in surprise; their roles had quickly reversed. Carly was the strong one now. She comforted him while he fell apart. Choked full of pain, Jake began, "I know she didn't want to—"

"Mr. Taylor?"

Jake's head darted up. A woman dressed in green scrubs stood in front of him. He swallowed deeply. "Yes?"

"I'm Doctor Holloway." She smiled briefly at him. "You'll be happy to know your wife is going to be all right. She suffered a mild concussion from the fall. Otherwise, there are no signs of additional injury. The trauma did cause her to go into premature labor, and we had some initial concerns, but we contacted her OB, and before we could do more then put on a pair of gloves, the baby came out kicking and screaming, probably thankful for his early release. He is a tiny guy, although doing well for entering this world almost eight weeks early. He's going to be with us for a while, but his lungs are strong, and that's always a good sign." She smiled. "Nurse McEntire will take you up to the nursery," she informed

185

him with a nod to the woman dressed in brightly colored scrubs next to her. "We should be transferring your wife to the postpartum ward within the hour. She may be a little drowsy from the sedatives she received, but I think I can allow her to visit with her husband for a few minutes. Nurse McEntire will take you to see her after you've been to the nursery."

"Thank you, Doctor." Jake released his breath in a heated rush. He reached out and shook the doctor's hand. "But I'm not Kimberly's hus—" He was interrupted by a targeted elbow into his ribs. "Thank you, Doctor Holloway," he amended and turned sharply to stare at Carly once the doctor walked away.

"Jake, please trust me on this and just go with it. It's not my place to explain, but I promise you that it will all make sense soon."

If the nurse overheard their exchange, she didn't acknowledge it. "If you'll follow me, I'll take you up to the nursery."

Jake and Carly followed the nurse through the pristine corridors in silence.

Kimberly would be all right. Jake felt like shouting his joy to the world. She and the baby were fine. The baby. The muscles in his back stiffened. He took a deep breath and tried to control the tension that flowed through him. Carly said to trust her and he would, at least until he had the chance to speak to Kimberly alone.

****

"He's so small."

"He is, isn't he?" Jake breathed in awe. He couldn't remember seeing something so tiny, so beautiful, so perfect. He pressed his face closer to the glass separating visitors from the newborns.

A nurse noticed Jake and Carly admiring the latest addition to the nursery, and she walked over to where the baby laid curled on his side, his eyes pressed shut in slumber. The nurse wheeled the portable crib closer to the glass pane. She smiled and turned to say something to another nurse in the room, before she walked to the nursery door.

"Excuse me, Mr. Taylor?"

Jake hated to drag his eyes away from the baby. He hated even more knowing he had to clear up the misunderstanding of his relationship to Kimberly and the baby. "Yes?"

"He's such a cutie, isn't he? He's doing great for a preemie. After we receive authorization from his pediatrician, we'll arrange for you to hold him. In the meantime, I hate to bother you, but we have some forms that we need your signature on, including your son's birth certificate form. It's the top paper."

The nurse pointed to an area down the hall. "There's a table and chairs over there. Just bring the forms back to the nursery when you're finished." The nurse smiled warmly and handed him the clipboard. "Your wife is in room 205. Dr. Holloway left word that she can receive visitors from immediate family, but only for a few minutes at a time."

"But you don't understand—"

"Take them, Jake."

Jake swung his head toward Carly, and his eyebrows shot up toward his hairline. He searched Carly's eyes, and she simply nodded.

Jake reached out and took the clipboard from the nurse. His hands trembled. His palms were damp with a layer of perspiration. What was going on? What in the hell was going on?

He glanced down at the clipboard in his hands, and his knees immediately went weak. He blinked rapidly, positive his eyes played tricks on him.

Certificate of Live Birth, it read. *Zachary Taylor Urbane. Mother: Kimberly Rose Urbane. Father: Jacob Samuel Taylor.* Jake felt his heart stop. "I, ah, how?"

"Come on, Jake. I think we better sit down." Carly placed her hand on his forearm and gently led him down the hall.

"I don't understand," Jake finally said once they were seated in a small alcove not far from the nursery. The clipboard of papers, the birth certificate form in particular, were the only things that kept him from believing he was caught in some bizarre dream.

"Jake, all I can tell you is what Kimberly told me when she first found out that she was pregnant, and that was that you are the baby's father. I believed her, and I've never had any reason to question her again."

"But—"

"Jake, anything else you want to know, you'll have to ask Kimberly herself." She paused and rose from her chair. "Now, that looks like a big stack of papers that need your signature. Why don't you get started on them while I go get us each a cup of coffee?" Carly smiled reassuringly at him and then provided him with a sisterly pat on the shoulder before she walked away.

Jake nodded automatically, but not before he realized he had done that a lot today, been ordered around and then nodded in acceptance. He had definitely lost his grip on reality.

Unable to help himself, his eyes drifted to the baby's birth certificate. Correction. His son's birth certificate, if Carly was to be believed. And if that was the case, he decided with fierce determination, then a few things on his son's birth certificate needed changing. Specifically, his name.

Kimberly had named their son after his grandfather, something that meant more to him than anything else she could have ever done for him. It was the baby's middle and last name that Jake had a serious issue with, one he corrected immediately. He scrawled a line through his son's name with quick precision, and with bold black letters, wrote Zachary Urbane Taylor. He would be damned if any child of his would not be a Taylor.

He spent several minutes staring at his son's name before he continued through the pile of forms, signing his name and changing his son's.

"Almost done?" Carly asked from behind him. She placed a large foam cup filled with coffee on the table for each of them.

"As a matter of fact, I'm signing the last one right...now." Jake scrawled his signature on the last form. He lifted his head, and the strong coffee aroma filled his senses. "Thanks for the coffee. I definitely need it." He took several large swallows of the hot drink before he placed his cup back down on the table.

"If you wouldn't mind returning these papers to the nurse, I think I'll visit Kimberly now."

"Sure."

Jake didn't miss the apprehension in her voice. She was nervous for her sister, and although he had lot of questions for Kimberly, Carly had no cause for worry. He loved Kimberly, probably never realized how much until now.

He handed Carly the clipboard with the birth certificate on top. Inevitably, she would see the blatant changes he had made to it, but he didn't care. Kimberly, and obviously everyone else, had decided that his child was not his concern. That was about to change. As of this moment, he silently vowed that he was in charge, of his son *and* Kimberly.

"I'll meet you back at the nursery. And Carly," he added before he walked away, "You don't need to worry about Kimberly. I'm not going to harm her. I love her too much to ever hurt her again." Jake walked away, and he realized for the first time in his life, he had rendered Carly Urbane speechless.

****

Jake knocked twice on the door before he opened it. His eyes immediately zeroed in on Kimberly.

Even though her eyes were closed, he could see the dark smudges beneath them. She had to be exhausted. She had been through so much over the last few hours.

Despite all she had been through, she looked beautiful lying against the stark white hospital sheets, her dark hair fanned against the pillow. He stared at her for several minutes, as an array of emotions soared through him.

One moment he wanted to rage at Kimberly, demanding to know why she had kept their child a secret from him, and then, a split second later he wanted to gather her into his embrace and never let her go.

He crossed the room and sat down in the chair next to her bed. His decision was made. Their hearts were going to win this time. He would make sure of it. Whatever her reasons were, and he was pretty sure he knew most of them, they no longer mattered. They were going to get through this, he silently vowed.

Jake took a deep breath. He ached to hold her hand in his own, to press a soft kiss on the inside of her wrist.

Kimberly's eyes fluttered open, and just as quickly closed, as she fought off the exhaustion consuming her. She slowly turned her head. She winced, and he realized that she likely battled the headache of a lifetime and even the briefest of movements had sent a searing pain throughout her head.

"Jake," she whispered to his bent head.

He was stooped over in the chair beside her bed, his head cradled in the palms of his hands, when he heard her voice call out his name, a soft caress against his skin.

He looked up at her. He was confused and uncertain, and his voice reflected it. "Kim."

Her beautiful brown eyes stared longingly at him, all the love she held for him for most of her life reflected in her gaze. He swallowed, hard.

"Jake," she began and winced at the pain that had to have come from hitting her head on the pavement.

"Kim, what is it? I'll call for the doctor." He started to stand when the soft command in her voice stopped him.

"No, it's all right. I just have a terrible headache. The nurse was in a little while ago and gave me something for it. I guess it just hasn't kicked in yet."

Jake's sigh of relief was audible. He reached out and brushed a strand of hair off of her forehead. She was in pain, and he was helpless to do anything but let her get some sleep. He should let her rest and come back later after she felt better. He told her as much, only to have her protest his suggestion.

"No, please, Jake. We need to talk about Zachary and... and everything," she whispered in a soft plea.

"Kim, you're in pain, you need to rest."

"No, I need to do this more. Jake," she began, only to stop when her tears began to cloud her eyes and clog her throat. "I'm sorry, ... I should have told you. I know that now. But I knew you would feel obligated to come home and take care of us, and I, I didn't want you to sacrifice yourself by being tied down to someone you didn't love just for the sake of our child. I couldn't do that to you, to any of us."

Jake wiped the tears from her cheeks with the pad of his thumb. He felt like he had just been punched in the stomach. "Kim." His eyes glistened with unshed tears. His foolish pride had brought them to this point, and he realized this hadn't been the first time. He had called himself a thousand times a fool over the last six months, and in his mind, it was well deserved. How could he have told her that he didn't love her, when he loved her more than life itself?

"Kim, please don't say you're sorry. You never were or will be just an obligation to me. I was wrong to leave you like I did." He grasped her hand into his own and clutched onto it like a lifeline.

"Jake—"

"No, please let me finish," he interrupted. "I need to tell you this, something I should have done six months ago." He took a deep, shuddering breath, "My feelings for you terrified me, Kim. I knew I could never repeat the life I had with my ex-wife. I couldn't survive that again. I wanted to believe you loved me as much as you said you did, but somewhere in my battered heart was a part of me that just refused to believe it. I refused to hope that we could have a future together."

"Jake. I told you—"

"Shh." He brushed away a strand of hair that had fallen across her cheek and then pressed his fingertips to her soft lips. "I have to say this. It's my fault you're lying here now, bruised and hurting, when instead, this should be the happiest day of your life."

He bent his head over their embraced hands and kissed her palm. "I love you." He kissed the inside of each of her wrists. "I love you, so much." His body shook with all the emotion he had finally allowed himself to release.

"Jake." She removed her hands from his and wrapped them around the back of his neck. "I love you too." She pulled him to her and hugged him tightly against her.

"I've been so afraid." Her voice cracked, and the sound shot through him like a knife to his heart. He pressed his eyes closed.

"I thought you would hate me for not telling you about the baby. Please forgive me, Jake. I was so confused."

"Kimberly." He opened his eyes and pulled himself out of her embrace to lower her back down against the pillows. She stared up at him expectantly, and he grasped each of her hands. "First of all, I could never hate you. I'll admit I was upset and more than a little confused when I left your house this afternoon. I still don't understand any of it, but I could never hate you. I love you, and that will never change." He bent over her and pressed a tender kiss to her lips, reluctant to pull away.

Kimberly's chestnut eyes sparkled back at him, and a smile curved her generous lips. He searched her face. His gaze wandered over her high cheek bones and finely arched brows. God, how he loved this woman.

"I was a little more than confused myself when the doctor informed me that I was pregnant, and not, by any stretch of the imagination, sick from a bad case of the flu." She looked up at him, and a pink stain colored her cheeks. "It was the last thing in the world I expected, but I suppose if I had known better, I would have recognized all the signs."

"I don't understand. The problems I had before, it doesn't make any sense."

"Maybe not, but according to the doctor, sometimes things just happen this way. He thought it was very likely that the mumps may have slowed things down a little, but not stopped them all together, if you know what I mean." She laughed softly, and her eyes lit up. "Whatever went wrong with your ex may have been a combination of both of your problems, not just yours, plus the stress of the whole situation. He said seeing on how we conceived this baby so quickly, we probably wouldn't have any problems in the future having more children."

Jake laughed out loud. "I'd like to make it official between us before we talk about having any more children. What do you think of a small ceremony with just our family as soon as we can break you and the baby out of here?"

"Jake Taylor, are you asking me to marry you?"

If Jake could have been any happier at the moment, he certainly didn't know how it could happen, and he hoped by the sheer joy that radiated from her that Kimberly felt the same way.

"You bet I am." He took her hand into his and squeezed it. "Kim." He sat up straighter and cleared his throat. "I'm asking you to marry me because I love you, no other reason. Only you. You know that, don't you?"

"I know. You're all I ever wanted, Jake. Every dream I've ever had has just come true. Having Zachary as part of that dream only makes it that more special. I love you."

Jake bent his head, intent to place a kiss on her inviting lips when a cough from somewhere near the doorway interrupted him.

"Ah, excuse me. How would the two of you like to meet your son?"

Jake recognized the nurse from the nursery and returned her smile. He looked down at Kimberly with all the love he had in the world, he hoped, reflected in his eyes.

Kimberly returned his look with one equally brimming with love. "We'd like that." She glowed with happiness. "We'd like that very much."

Chapter 17

"Happy birthday to you. Happy birthday, dear Zachary, happy birthday to you!"

A round of applause, mixed with laughter, filled the room as five-year-old Zachary blew out the candles on his cake. "What a big boy you are, honey," Kimberly cooed to her son.

"Jake, please grab Cameron and put him on your lap. Zane, hold on to Noah. That way I can get all the Taylor men in the picture," Kimberly directed from behind the lens of her camera.

Jake and Zane exchanged knowing glances over the children's heads. Jake mouthed "sorry" to his brother, even though they both knew they were stuck doing the impossible. Trying to control two squirming kids, with a third stuffing cake in his mouth, were beyond each of their abilities.

"Kimberly, I don't mean to spoil your fun," Zane paused, and then smiled for another photo before he continued, "but I have a wet nephew on my lap, and he's getting wetter."

"All right, that's enough for now," she agreed and placed her camera down on the patio table. "Jake, I'll take Cameron and change his diaper, if you'll clean up Zachary. You've got Noah, Zane."

Jake watched Kimberly smile at their oldest son, his face smeared with chocolate icing from the tip of his nose to the bottom of his chin and sighed. There was no way she could resist, and she didn't, when she picked up her camera and snapped several more shots of her sons.

Each of the older Taylor brothers groaned simultaneously before Jake spoke up, "Kim, you've taken enough photographs for three albums this afternoon. And honey, Cameron is really wet."

"You're welcome to change him." The sweet sound of her laughter filled the room. "You too, Uncle Zane."

"No way, not me." Zane held up his hands in protest. "I'll clean up Noah's face and hands, but that's as far as it goes for me. Favorite uncle I may be, but diaper changer I am not."

"I heard that, Zane, and you are not their favorite Uncle," came a shout from the kitchen.

Kimberly, Jake, and Zane all laughed in unison. It had been an ongoing argument between George and Zane since the birth of Zachary as to who was ultimately the favorite uncle. After the birth of Cameron, the competition became even fiercer, and to the boy's good fortune, it became a competition of which uncle could outdo the other in both gifts and attention.

"Are not!" Zane shouted back. He picked up Noah, and Jake hoisted Zachary under his arm.

"If we only had one son, I could understand the competition between you and George. But there's three of these little guys, plenty to go around." Jake laughed and patted his brother on the back when they entered the nursery.

"I wonder if they would fight like this over our daughters?" Kimberly commented with a challenging eyebrow in their direction. She laid eighteen-month-old Cameron down on the changing table, while Jake used a wet wipe on Zachary's face before he passed him to his brother. He bent down and repeated the action with Noah.

Zane picked out a clean shirt for his oldest nephew, and Jake noticed that Zane intentionally passed over one that had been a present from George. Instead,

Zane put the boy in a jersey that Zane had given to him for Christmas the previous year. Jake shook his head. His brother never changed.

"Yeah, well, we're done having kids, so it looks like we'll never know, right Kimberly?" Jake stared meaningfully in her direction. His smile grew, until Kimberly looked up from the changing table and smiled coyly at him. Oh, no, he knew that expression. Knew it all too well.

"Kimberly, don't even say it. Don't even say it," Jake looked at his wife and then over at his brother. His gaze shot back over to his wife. His eyes grew wide.

"Actually, there's something I've been meaning to tell you, Jake."

"Whoa. I'm out of here," Zane choked out between gasps of laughter. "Come on Zack, Noah. Let's hit it." He placed Noah on his hip and grabbed Zachary's hand. The trio raced out of the room; Zane's laughter echoed behind him.

"Kim." Jake groaned although he couldn't keep the smile from creeping upward on his lips. "Tell me you're kidding? Please, tell me you're kidding?" He reached out and grabbed his wife around the waist after making sure Cameron played safely with some blocks in the corner of the room.

"'Fraid not." She circled her arms around his neck and pulled his head down to hers. "Jake," she whispered between several passionate kisses. "I think a girl would be nice this time, don't you?"

About Lisa Lanay

Lisa began reading romance novels during high school. Since then, she has read thousands of romances, preferring a splash of humor throughout the story line and, of course, a happy ending. She began writing stories in her head over twenty years ago and finally decided to open up her laptop and record them. Today, her characters love nothing more than to play out their stories while she walks on the beach or is on an airplane - so if you happen to see her in either place, make sure to ask her for introductions to the characters in her next book - but be prepared to stop and have a glass of wine with her, as she will undoubtedly want to bounce ideas off of you.

Lisa's family rescued *Lady* from the 'dog pound' in the 70's and *Bosco* soon followed. Today, she has many family members and friends that volunteer at shelters, give their time toward rescue efforts, and who are proud owners of rescue dogs. Lisa includes rescue dogs in each of her books in hopes of conveying the joy and love that comes from rescuing. While she considers Doberman Pinschers to be the true dog love of her life, she is the proud mommy of a Boxer, whom she adopted from her elderly parents when they were no longer able to care for her. Lisa hopes to rescue a Doberman Pinscher... or maybe two someday.

Follow Lisa Lanay @lisalanayauthor on Instagram & Facebook

Preview Taming Zane by Lisa Lanay

Coming Fall 2019

Chapter One

Shannon stowed her carry-on bag in the airplane's overhead compartment and then sank into her seat with a sigh of relief. It was a window seat, and so far, she was the only one seated in her row. Fifteen minutes until takeoff. Perhaps her luck would hold out, and she would have the whole row to herself. The latest best-seller in her hand, a blanket on her lap, and a half-way decent movie was more than enough to entertain her for the four-hour trip from Chicago to San Francisco. As long as they didn't experience any turbulence (and even the thought of a bumpy ride sent panic from her stomach to her toes), the long flight she had been dreading earlier may not be so bad after all. She had so little time in her life to curl up with a good book that even on an airplane, it was a welcome reprieve from her normally hectic schedule.

"Mom. Mom! Over here, I found our seats. There's a lady sitting by the window, and you said I could sit by the window."

A harried looking woman with a squirming toddler balanced on her hip trailed several feet behind a rambunctious little boy. "Hold on, honey, don't put anything down yet. Let's turn around, and I will speak with the flight attendant. Maybe there's a chance we can get a row to ourselves."

Shannon released the breath she hadn't realized she'd been holding, until the moment her lungs exhaled in relief. Mother, son, and baby cramped into the two seats next to her? No. No. No. There had to be some vacant rows still open on the large airplane. She turned in her seat to make a quick scan of the rows behind her, and her hopes of an enjoyable trip, vanished.

"Come on, please, let there be an open row for them." She clutched the seat's arm rest, and as discreetly as she could with her neck craned at a one-hundred-and-eighty-degree angle, she watched the flight attendant seat her would-be travel companions several rows behind her.

"Whew, was that close." Glad that mini crisis was averted, she giggled to herself. She loved kids, but on a plane, and when they weren't her own, she preferred not to be crammed into a small space with them. She was reminded of her own son, who was leaving for Disney World that evening with her parents. She grabbed her cell phone to call him, and just as quickly, stopped herself short. Ethan had promised to remain within his grandparents' sights at all times, especially at the parks, and in return, she had agreed not to constantly check up on him. She was determined to live up to her end of her bargain, even if it practically killed her to do it. Shannon stared at her phone screen for several seconds before she turned the cell off and placed it inside of her purse. Eager to get comfortable again for the long flight, she snuggled deep into her seat and picked up her book.

"Hopefully there won't be anyone in the middle seat. That would be nice."

Startled to hear a voice that seemed to come from right next to her, Shannon's eyes flew up from the pages of her book. She turned her head, and to her shock, she found herself gazing into a pair of eyes the color of the sky on a clear summer day, and they happened to be in the very attractive face of the man seated in the aisle seat of her row, a mere two seats away. She recalled seeing him in the gate area earlier and thinking he was attractive, but now, up close and next to her, she realized he was smoking hot! She would definitely have to thank the flight attendant for making this switch in seating arrangements.

"I, ah, yeah. Me too." Discreetly as she could with her mouth gaping open, she checked out her new row companion from head to toe. *Oh wow!* Not only were those baby blues to die for, but they were part of a face that could not have been any better if it were on the cover of her now forgotten book. Dark, thick eyebrows slashed across a forehead that was creased with the faintest of wrinkles. Okay, so his good looks placed him in the same group as some of her handsome male students, the ones who left their female companions in tears at least once during the college semester. Still, it wasn't as if she was going to jump the guy's bones; she just planned to admire him for a few hours. Where was the harm in that? Besides, she had already been down that road years ago and had the broken heart to prove it. She had had almost eight years to learn from her bad judgement in men, and she had no plans to repeat the experience. In her opinion, great looking guys always caused nothing but trouble.

"I think boarding is done," he returned with a grin. "I'd really appreciate an uneventful flight. Although, I overhead a flight attendant say that we might experience some bumps along the way."

"Yes, I heard that also. Unfortunately, I'm not a big fan of turbulence." She shot him a slight smile, and immediately her cheeks burned to a bright pink. Oh, how lame could she get? She brought her lower lip between her teeth. Can't you think of anything more interesting to say than your fear of turbulence? She straightened in her seat and widened her smile. Was there really a great-looking guy making small talk, seated in the same row with her, and with no wedding ring in sight? Her current circumstances were way better than the plot of the book she had discarded moments ago. A zing of excitement shot through her, despite the warning bells ringing loud and clear inside her head.

"At least it's a non-stop flight to San Francisco," she finally added, and then stifled the groan that rose in her throat. So much for him finding her to be an interesting conversationalist. You sure blew that one, Shannon.

She tried to tear her eyes away from him, but they seemed to be stuck in place. She watched him place a battered backpack under the seat in front of him, without much regard to its contents, before he buckled the safety belt around his trim waist. The fabric of his black T-shirt, clung to his thick arms and chest, before it disappeared into a pair of faded jeans. Shannon pulled her lower lip between her teeth again and then swallowed nervously as she continued to stare at him.

He sat back in his seat, and her gaze remained fixed on him as he turned his head toward her with a smile on his generous lips. "I don't know if I could take another connection. My trip from Kilimanjaro had enough connections to last me a very long time."

Shannon tore her gaze from what she saw were tiny gray strands, mixed in with the rest of his charcoal hair, to stare back at him. "You flew to Chicago from Kilimanjaro?" Her eyes widened, and her brows arched over them, high on her forehead. She had always wanted to travel to foreign countries, but taking care of an active seven-year-old and working a full-time job that often required sixty hours a week kept her from going to the grocery store most days, let alone traveling abroad.

Her new row companion flipped through an airline magazine before he placed it on the seat between the two of them, and she noticed that his fingers were long, his nails buffed to a dull sheen. Okay, so she'd seen more rugged hands on a guy, but really, who was she to judge? The guy cared about his appearance, better than grease stains under his nails, she reasoned.

"I left two days ago, and after numerous delays and a few senseless connections, here I am. Finally, one flight away from San Francisco, and home."

"Kilimanjaro, wow," she breathed, in little more than a whisper. "Were you there on business?"

"I guess you could call it that." His eyes were pensive, and he shrugged. "Excuse me, a second." He sent another quick smile in her direction, before he turned to capture the attention of a passing flight attendant.

"Hi, there. Any chance of an extra magazine?"

Shannon saw him flash the flight attendant a brilliant smile, and based on her glowing reaction, Shannon bet the woman would return with a whole stack of magazines, and then offer to sit on his lap and read them to him.

"Why sure. *Time* or *Newsweek,* okay?" came her reply in a sultry tone that Shannon knew she had not used with the passenger seated behind them when he had asked the same question only minutes ago. I bet he flashes those hypnotizing eyes all the time, she mused, totally unaware of the powerful effect they had on women. Irritation flared within her as she watched their exchange with something akin to envy, right before she realized that she would have retrieved the magazines for him herself, had he asked her.

"How about something lighter? *People* perhaps? I've had enough of the real world to keep me going for a while." He returned the flight attendant's gaze with another dazzling smile.

"Sure thing, Sugar, I'll be right back." The flight attendant held his gaze, which made her interest in him more than obvious.

"Thanks, darlin'."

Sugar? Darlin'? All right, she admitted, the flight attendant had one of those cute Southern accents you couldn't fake without sounding ridiculous, but really, S*ugar*? And *Darlin'*? He had just called her darlin', and she appeared to bask in the endearment, giggling like a schoolgirl when she walked away. Shannon started to roll her eyes upward and stopped herself. What was going on with her? The guy was obviously a natural charmer, and even though she had been seated next to him for less than five minutes, and she had already staked her claim on him, prepared to warn any potential competition to back off. Wait, hadn't she just reminded herself that hot guys were off limits to her? Hadn't she just mentally reprimanded herself? About five minutes ago, and counting, and this time, she did roll her eyes.

"Sorry about that... ah. What was... what was I saying?"

He turned, and his attention was focused on her again. *Oh man*, no wonder the flight attendant giggled. A pair of dimples winked at her from each corner of his mouth, and she had to stop herself from reaching out and touching each one of them with her fingertips.

"You, ah, were about to explain to me why you were in Kilimanjaro?" How could one man be so handsome? It just wasn't fair. She'd take a guy with half his looks and be content for the rest of her life. Okay, maybe not half, but close enough, she thought, in case Cupid and staff took mercy and listened to her thoughts.

"You're right, good memory. Anyway, I'm a plastic surgeon, specializing in reconstructive surgery," he replied with a shrug. "I donate at least a few weeks a year in third world or war-torn, countries, doing what I can to help medically. This time it was in an area about forty-five miles outside of Kilimanjaro."

"Oh, wow," Shannon replied, when she could finally find her voice. How did she respond to that one? Did she praise him for such a noble contribution to society, or did she try to impress him with some comment about Kilimanjaro? But what about Kilimanjaro? In fact, where was Kilimanjaro? It was no small wonder that years ago, her college advisor strongly suggested she swap out a global studies class for a psych class, before she had the chance to flunk out.

With a slight shake of her head, she gladly diverted her attention from her limited world knowledge back to the gorgeous man next to her. A reconstructive plastic surgeon who donated his time to victims in third-world countries? With a face and body to kill for? Was this some kind of practical joke? This guy was too good to be true, and he was seated next to her for the next four hours. No way. Nothing like this ever happened to her. Not her, not Shannon McGregor.

Over the last several years she had endured endless hours of girlfriends bragging about some wonderful guy they had met at work, or the health club, or on the train, or anywhere else gorgeous hunks seemed to hang out, which seemed to be everywhere she was not. Actually, though she hated to admit it, most of her friends were now married to these alleged hunks. Meanwhile, she spent her life as a college professor, meeting men either so young they called her ma'am or so old they referred to her as a youngster. Huh. She had finally met someone exciting enough to brag about to her girlfriends, even if her time with him was only the duration of a plane flight.

"How did you decide on Kilimanjaro? I mean, nothing against Kilimanjaro," she quickly added. "I was just wondering how you know where you are needed?" Great, he probably thinks I'm some country bumpkin who has never been out of her hometown, which was not that far off the mark. Outside of traveling to nearby Wisconsin on family vacations, she rarely left the Chicagoland area. This flight was her first one in over six years, and although she considered Chicago one of the most interesting cities in the world, according to her very biased opinion, it was only one city in a world of thousands, most of which she had never visited.

She watched him chuckle under his breath, and she thought he must have heard the question numerous times before in the past. "Actually, Kilimanjaro found me. I'm listed in a database of doctors willing to volunteer for extended international assignments. I'm single and don't have any family ties. Fortunately, I might add," he stopped to chuckle before he continued. "My time is my own. Typically, a group of us go together as a team of medical professionals, often as part of the same team every year. I and several of the doctors and nurses spend most of the year on staff for various hospitals throughout the country and are provided with the flexibility to leave when duty calls. The hospitals typically don't mind the good PR." Although it was an explanation he probably recited often, Shannon picked up on the passion in his voice and saw the way his eyes lit up when he spoke of his volunteer work.

"I think it's amazing that each of you is willing to go where ever you are needed. That's wonderful and very commendable." She tried to volunteer for numerous charitable causes, she even donated blood regularly, but she sure didn't travel to foreign countries to save the world.

"Thanks. While I find my day job rewarding, I think it's important to push myself outside of the hospital, and the comforts of San Francisco, and into the reality of what others, especially children which I try to help as much as possible, are dealing with globally. It's easy to get wrapped up in your own world, especially if you like that world." The corner of one side of his mouth titled upward, and his eyes reflected a tint of humor.

Shannon stared back at him and felt something akin to a punch to her gut. Her skin felt warm, and she knew a deep blush must be staining her cheeks as her admiration for new row mate grew exponentially. He might be handsome, and a very skilled flirt, but he also seemed to be a very good guy. She swallowed a gulp of air and reminded herself that she had also thought Ethan's dad was a really good guy and he had been, right until the day she had told him she was pregnant.

"Anyway, enough about me. What brings you to San Fran?"

Before she could answer, the flight attendant she had waspishly nicknamed Scarlet O'Hara returned with his magazines, her hips sashaying with an annoyingly blatant invitation.

"Here you are, the last two issues of *People*. Now you need anything else, you just let me know," she told him in the same sugary Southern drawl she had used previously. She added a wink, and Shannon knew that it meant she'd be glad to go beyond the call of duty for her gorgeous passenger.

Shannon was tempted to mimic a gagging gesture, when, just in the nick of time, she realized that her hunky companion was no longer looking at the flight attendant, but instead, stared boldly at her.

"You were about to explain why you're on your way to San Francisco," he prompted with a raise of a brow, coupled with a grin that left her insides melted into major mush.

Shannon felt a blush creep up her cheeks, infinitely grateful he couldn't read her thoughts about the flight attendant a minute ago. Normally she didn't have a waspish bone in her body, but there was something about her traveling companion that brought out a mixture of emotions in her, most of them ones she knew she could do without.

"I, uh, am going for part vacation, part work. I have an interview at the end of the week with Stanford University regarding a research project I'm working on. The university I'm on staff at as a professor in Chicago ran out of money for the project when it was only half completed." She looked down at her hands and then turned her gaze upward to find he continued to stare at her. Had any man ever focused this much attention on her, especially when she discussed her work? Not by a long-shot. "I'm interviewing with several schools in hopes that one of them will be able to fund the remainder of the research. If Stanford comes through with the grant, it would mean I would need to relocate for at least a year. The opportunity comes with a faculty position, which makes it practically perfect. I decided that since I've never even been to

California, or the west coast, that it would be a good idea to spend some time in the area."

"I agree," he chuckled. "It sounds as if it's a pretty big decision to make, and it's important to know what you're getting yourself into."

"Yeah. My family and friends think I'm crazy for even considering it, especially because I'm not exactly the type to get up and move half way across the country, but this research project is really important to me." She paused and took a deep breath. "And while I want to finish the project, I have to agree with everyone else. Moving is kind of scary. I've always lived in Chicago, and well, I know change can be good, but I'm comfortable there."

"Sometimes we have to break away from our safety nets and follow our dreams."

Shannon assumed he spoke from experience. "Is that what you've done?"

"Many times."

"Really? And it always worked out?"

His eyes darkened and became distant. "No. Actually they... I mean—" He shook his head and chuckled. Small creases appeared at the corners of each of his eyes. "Like I said earlier, it's important to know what you're getting into before you do it."

Shannon was tempted to ask him to explain what he originally set out to say, when he set his magazine down and reached his hand out to her.

"By the way, I'm Zane. Zane Taylor."

She placed her hand in his and a nervous giggle slipped from her lips. "I'm Shannon. Shannon McGregor." She was tempted to add, "Single, and very available college professor from Chicago who just felt a thousand tiny bolts of electricity from the mere contact of your hand." But she didn't. Reluctantly, she removed her hand from his grasp, and the sensation of his touch continued to linger on her skin.

209

"Nice to meet you Shannon. What type of research are you conducting? Or is it something so highly confidential that you can't share it with me?" The beginning of a smile curved the corners of his mouth.

Shannon laughed out loud at the idea. "Not hardly. Unless you consider the potential impact of a patient's emotional health status with the progression of Lewy Body Dementia top secret. Pretty boring for most people."

"Not at all. It's sounds interesting. Why the topic?"

Shannon had to stop herself from squirming in her seat. He appeared so genuinely interested in her work, she wanted to reach out and throw her arms around his neck and scream, thank you! Men, particularly the ones who her friends swore were perfect for her, and never were, rarely showed interest in her work. "My grandfather suffered from Lewy Body Dementia. It was awful. After watching him struggle with it, both mentally and physically, I decided that there needed to be more research conducted on the subject."

Zane's eyes narrowed ever so slightly, and she felt nervous under his scrutiny.

"Good for you," he finally said. "Passion is a powerful motivator. So few people have enough of it."

Shannon's eyes widened, and she wondered whether they were still discussing her work. "Ah, yeah, I agree." A strand of his black hair fell against his forehead and she had to force herself to stop from reaching out and pushing it aside. She gulped and cracked a smile despite the tremor she felt crawl against her skin.

"How far along are you in—"

"Headsets for the movie? Headsets?" The flight attendant shot a questioning glance in their direction.

Zane was the first to break eye contact, and Shannon quickly followed his lead.

"Sure," Zane replied.

Shannon nodded, unable to find her voice.

"What movie are they playing?" he asked with a slight turn of his head in the flight attendant's direction.

Here we go again Shannon thought, Scarlett O'Hara in full throttle. He was hers, she wanted to yell in frustration.

"You're in luck this morning. Since we're having problems with the audio for the news clip we usually play after the movie, we're going to try to squeeze in two movies instead. Two old favorites, *Home Again* and *Family Man*. The first movie will be starting in a few minutes." The flight attendant smiled warmly, although she was obviously put out when Zane gave her a swift thank you and returned his attention back to Shannon.

Shannon provided the flight attendant with a brief smile, making sure it conveyed everything she was thinking, specifically to back off of Mr. Hunky.

"Well, I haven't heard of either, so I hope they're comedies, and not some sappy chick flicks."

"There is nothing wrong with chick flicks, and as for the movies being comedies, chick flicks all the way. It looks like you're out of luck, after all." Shannon chuckled, and silently added, so am I. She pressed her hand to her stomach in hopes to ease the nervous flutter inside. Sitting through two romantic movies, with a guy who could have been a movie star himself, would be nothing short of sheer torture, requiring every ounce of willpower she possessed. With a defeated sigh, she smiled weakly at Zane and then put on her earphones.

By the time the second movie ended, Zane had finished his second scotch and water, and Shannon had witnessed him squirm in his seat more than once.

"Those movies were so good," she said purposely to gauge his reaction. She might not have a lot of experience with men, but she could spot a guy that was not in the market for a committed relationship. With his looks, he was probably a renowned playboy, a confirmed bachelor who planned to stay that way.

"Ugh."

"What? You don't think that a good-looking, successful guy, who shuns commitment, could be happy to wake up one day and find himself with a wife, two kids and a mortgage, his past life completely wiped away by a glimpse of how one choice changed his entire life?"

Zane's stared back at her with eyebrows shot up near his hairline and his eyes filled with mock fear. "Not hardly. What guy would?"

Shannon's smile widened. Despite his acknowledgement of his confirmed bachelorhood, it didn't deter her from drooling over him, no matter how much her conscience warned her to keep her distance. The last thing she needed in her life was heartbreak over a guy who was in a relationship for the good times only. She had had one of those already, and it was enough to last her several life times. Not that there was a snowball's chance in hell that Dr. Zane Taylor would ever be interested in her, but a girl could have her fantasies, couldn't she?

"Yeah, I guess you're right." Her smile widened until she spied her tote bag and a slip of paper sticking out from in it. "Oh, I can't believe I forgot to show this to you between movies, and now we're landing. Darn it." She tossed her long hair, to behind her shoulder. She reached into her tote bag and pulled out several sheets of folded paper.

"Since you're from San Francisco, would you mind taking a quick look at my list? It's a list of recommended tourist spots I found on some travel sites. Stanford's website also suggested some neighborhoods for housing in the area. I'd really appreciate it."

Shannon caught Zane staring at her hair and secretly smiled to herself. She had been told that her hair was one of her better attributes, and Zane's look of admiration reinforced it. She was excited by the possibility that the attraction was mutual.

Zane shook his head. "Ah, sure." He grinned and took the list from her outstretched hand. "Not bad," he commented after he studied the list for a few minutes. "You've definitely covered all the tourist traps. Man, it's been years since I've been to some of these places," he muttered. "You live somewhere, and eventually you take for granted what others travel there to see." He ran his hand along the bottom of his chin.

"I feel the same way about Chicago."

Zane glanced up from the paper to look at her. "I don't get to Chicago often, haven't been there in years. But I get it."

She nodded. "You should visit, especially in the summer. Chicago is great, there is always something going on."

He bent his head slightly and continued to watch her. "Maybe, I'll do that sometime soon."

Shannon pulled her lower lip between her teeth, and he grinned back at her.

"Do you have a pen? I typically have three or four in my bag, but they all seemed to have disappeared on this trip."

"Thanks." He took the pen from her without looking up. He made a hasty scribble to the top of one of the pages and then handed them back to her.

"It's my cell phone number." He winked and then smiled. "I used a realtor a few years ago that has experience with the Palo Alto area. Rather than have you spend an entire day driving around in an unfamiliar area, I think it would be a lot easier for you to contact me once I'm home, and I can locate her business card."

"Oh. Thanks." It didn't take much for her to realize that she was disappointed by his explanation, but what had she expected? An offer to be her tour guide for the day? To show her Palo Alto himself? Hardly, she silently admonished. After all, she was simply Shannon McGregor, Midwest college professor with a rather mundane life, while he was sexy, single, doctor extraordinaire, who traveled around the world and was most likely on his way home to a handful of equally sexy, and exciting, girlfriends. Just another chapter in her life that had ended uneventfully. She folded her list and stuck it in the middle of her novel before she placed both inside her tote bag.

"Who knows?" A devilish gleam, radiated from his eyes. "I haven't been to Alcatraz in years, and there's always talk of plans to close the old prison in the not too far future. More likely a rumor to entice tourism, but you never know. Perhaps I'll join you on one of the tours; I haven't played tourist in a long time."

Shannon was about to blurt out, "When?" but stopped herself just in the nick of time. She needed to get a grip on her reaction to him before she started sounding desperate, something she never would have been accused of prior to meeting him. There was just something about him. Something? How about a million things, she inwardly sighed.

"That would be great." She moistened her lips with the tip of her tongue. "I'll make sure to text you once I'm settled in." Oh well, she could dream, couldn't she? Who knows, maybe she would get up the nerve to invite him to spend the day with her? Stranger things have happened, she acknowledged, with a little jolt to her heart.

Zane removed his seat belt as soon as the pilot announced it was safe to do so. "Well, it was a pleasure to meet you, Shannon McGregor, despite your incredibly bad taste in movies." He winked at her and stood up.

"You too, Zane. Oh, and thanks for your help with my list."

"My pleasure." He gave her another heart-stopping smile, and she barely stopped herself from drooling. Control yourself Shannon, he's not your type remember? Gorgeous, successful, and oh yeah, likely no interest in a commitment lasting longer this weekend. Definitely not your type.

Zane turned to look at her when the row in front of them began to disembark, and she remained buckled in her seat. "Have you decided to stay on the plane?"

"Not hardly." Shannon quickly gestured to the overhead space several rows behind them. "My suitcase is a few rows back, so I need to wait until this section clears out." Besides, she had another suitcase to retrieve from baggage claim, so she wasn't in the rush Zane seemed to be, and she couldn't blame him. If she had spent the last two days traveling like he had, she would have pushed her way through the crowded plane to the exit door.

He settled his backpack across his shoulder and retrieved his duffle bag from the overhead compartment. "I guess this is goodbye, for now. Don't forget to text me. You'd like Palo Alto, and it's been years since I've had the chance to play tourist, and certainly never with such an attractive companion."

Zane gave her with one last smile before he turned and walked away and now, moments later, Shannon could still feel the heat of his deep blue eyes caressing her face. He had called her attractive, and while she wanted to believe it, she also knew that he probably said the same thing to everyone woman he met. She watched as he walked down the aisle, and she felt her heart sink with every step he took toward the exit.

During the brief break between movies, she had questioned him about his work and the places he traveled. He had been to countries she had never heard of and performed surgeries that were nothing short of miracles, and he talked in a way that made her realize he considered it just an ordinary day's work, rather than the big deal that she knew other people would make of it. She had been completely taken back when he asked so many questions about her own career. His interest in her research made her feel special, as if her work was as equally important as his own, something that rarely happened with any of the numerous men she had met over the years.

Shannon experienced a strange sensation that started in the pit of her stomach, traveled up to her throat, and by the time it arrived in her mouth, was a giant knot of pain. Zane

Taylor was the most exciting and attractive man she had ever met, and he had just walked off the plane and out of her life. He would return to what she imagined to be the exciting life of a surgeon and world traveler, while she would play tourist for a few days and then go back to her life of mother and college professor. He wouldn't remember her by the time his Uber picked him up, and she would have to force herself to forget him months from now.

She recalled the way his deep blue eyes lit up when he told her a story and how his dimples winked at her when he laughed. Zane Taylor was all male, all gorgeous male, indeed. She stopped daydreaming to look around her and noticed that the plane was nearly empty. She unbuckled her seatbelt with an exaggerated sigh. She'd just have to block him out of her mind and concentrate on her plans for the day. She gathered her things from the seat, slung her tote bag over her shoulder, and retrieved her bag from the overhead compartment. She shook her head. Try to forget Zane Taylor? Yeah, right.

48969323R00134

Made in the USA
San Bernardino, CA
19 August 2019